Shadows beneath the Shore::

Secrets of a Dominican Mine

Victor Acosta

Shadows Beneath the Shore:

Secrets of a Dominican Mine

ISBN: 979-8-3484-7855-1

Published in the United States of America.

www.victoracosta.com

For my grandmother and my heroine Silveria Uribe "Bella" for inspiring me throughout my life. You always used to say "El Mundo Pertenece a Los Valientes" The world belongs to the Brave and I couldn't agree more with you. I decided to write this book to honor your memory and testimony that nothing is impossible, we all have to be brave like you.

My daughters Gigi, Lisamarie, Jessie, and Kristen love you with all my heart I hope this novel makes you girls proud of your dad.

My Mom and Dad thank you for giving me life and unconditional love.

My wife Paula thank you for believing in me and making me a better man for every breath I take next to you.

Shadows Beneath the Shore:
Secrets of a Dominican Mine

Victor Acosta

PROLOGUE

Tony Costa is an ordinary high school senior, but his life takes a dramatic turn as he graduates. His father, Mario, wanting to give him a memorable graduation present, plans a trip to the Dominican Republic for Tony and his mother. However, the journey takes an unexpected turn when Tony learns of his father's sudden death, later revealed by his godfather to be not just an accident but something far more sinister.

With a heavy heart, Tony sets out on a journey to uncover the truth about his father's death and his family's past. It was not an ordinary death but one shrouded in mystery and deceit. And so, with a determination to uncover the truth, he embarks on a quest that will take him from the bustling cities of Italy to the rugged, untamed wilderness of the Caribbean through his grandfather's journals.

Tony soon finds himself on a journey to uncover the truth of his family's past. This journey will take him along the way; he learns about his grandfather Antonio Rossi, a young soldier who defected from the Italian army during WWII, and Mario Rossi, Antonio's brother, a graduate geologist with an unquenchable thirst for knowledge.

As Tony uncovers the truth about his family's past, he discovers that his grandfather and great-uncle Mario were geologists and mining entrepreneurs who had a mining operation in the Dominican Republic. They explored, researched, and perfected the mining of Amber. And the truth about Mario's death might be connected to their mining operation.

1

CHAPTER

The rain outside Tony's apartment in the Bronx mirrored the storm of emotions raging within him. As he sat by the window, gazing at the raindrops trickling down the glass, memories of his father flooded his mind. The ache of loss was an unrelenting companion, a weight that Tony carried in the depths of his being. He traced the edges of his father's photograph, the smile frozen in time, and wondered if he'd ever uncover the truth behind his death.

"I missed him so much," Tony whispered to himself, his voice barely audible against the drumming rain. The room seemed to echo with the solitude of his grief.

The rain intensified a relentless rhythm that matched the cadence of Tony's thoughts. He couldn't escape the regret that clawed at him, the haunting notion that different choices might have preserved the warmth of his father's presence.

His memory painted vivid scenes of their last trip together. The laughter, the shared adventures, and the bond between father and son were etched into his head. Tony's fingers lingered over his dad's picture as if the touch could bring those moments back to life.

"If we hadn't gone, he would still be here with us," Tony mused, his gaze fixed on the rain-streaked window. The words lingered in the air, heavy with the weight of an unanswerable 'what if.'

The recollection of his father's memory was a double-edged sword. It provided solace, a reminder of the love they had shared, but it also deepened the ache of absence. The rawness of the loss felt as if time had stood still, frozen in the moment when his father had left.

The room, dimly lit by the overcast sky, became a sanctuary of introspection. Tony's internal dialogue continued a silent conversation with the ghost of the past. "His memory is so vivid; it's like it was just taken recently," he confessed, his voice catching on the edges of sorrow.

In the solitude of his grief, Tony wrestled with the pain that refused to dull. The photograph of his father, smiling and alive, was a testament to a love that transcended the boundaries of time and space.

"The pain of missing him is still palpable," Tony acknowledged his words a whispered admission. The rain outside seemed to weep in harmony with his lament, a shared symphony of sorrow.

The room held the sacred echoes of a son grappling with the enormity of his loss. As the rain continued its melancholic dance, Tony closed the family picture album, knowing that within those pages, his father's spirit would forever reside.

2

CHAPTER

On my way home from school, chatting with Oscar and Luis, "I'm so excited for my spring break trip to DR," I commented with a wide smile.

"Hey, Tony! JUMP! The train is coming." Luis Yelled. As the screeching sound of the C train approaches 50th Street Station, I desperately look for my subway pass in my bookbag. "Wait. Wait. I can't find my pass.", I yelled back.

"JUMP!" yelled Oscar in a mocking manner.

"It's Oscar crazy? he wants me to jump the turnstiles and get in trouble." I whispered to myself while my heart pounded in my chest, I could feel it beating faster and faster, and my breathing was suddenly more intense. The train opens the door, and I hear the conductor; "59th Street Station next".

I go for it while Oscar and Luis hold the door for me; the booth teller yells out of his lungs, "PAY YOUR FARE," as I run like lighting inside the train.

Luis breaks into laughter. "Hahaha."

"¿Qué pasa pues? are you scared?" Says Oscar in his Colombian accent.

Terrified about what I had done and knew my mom would kill me if she ever found out. "What are you talking about? Didn't you see me running? I'm just tired; leave me alone." I replied.

"So why are you going to The Dominican Republic, again to do what?" Says Luis.

As I catch my breath, we walk toward the front of the train. "I'm going to meet my aunt Maria for the first time and a few cousins; besides, my dad thinks it is a good graduation present."

"…Wow," said Luis

"…so, the whole family is going; I didn't know you were a Jevito". Hinting that my family has money to pamper me.

"My dad will catch up with us later, something with some test material he had to prepare at work."

My dad is Mario Costa, a faculty member at Columbia University who teaches Geology. The week before our trip, he said he was preparing some exams for his class and would meet with us the following week in Santo Domingo, the Capital of the Dominican Republic, where my family comes from, a small, divided island in the Caribbean.

Oscar smirks, "Well, look at Mr. Fancy Pants here, flying off to the Caribbean to meet the family and all."

I chuckle, trying to shake off the tension from the turnstile escapade, "Yeah, yeah. A graduation present, but I heard there's more to it. You know how dads are, always mysterious."

Luis grins, "Your dad's a professor, right? What's he teach?"

"Geology," I reply. "He's into rocks and stuff. Pretty cool, I guess."

Oscar raises an eyebrow, "Geology? Sounds like a snooze fest."

I defend my dad's passion, "It's more interesting than you think. He's always talking about these rocks with weird names. Amber, I think, is his latest obsession."

"Amber?" Luis echoes. "Isn't that the stuff with the bugs trapped inside, like in Jurassic Park?"

"Yeah, exactly!" I nod. "He's been researching mines in the Dominican Republic, apparently. Some family business or whatever."

Oscar's eyes widen, "Mines? Like, gold mines?"

"I think so," I reply, "And something about Amber being a big deal. He's been in touch with some relatives we never knew existed. It's like a family reunion or something."

Luis raises an eyebrow, "So, you're, what, like, royalty over there?"

I laugh, "Far from it. Probably just regular folks, but it'll be interesting to see where Dad comes from. And who knows, maybe there's a hidden treasure waiting for me."

The train rumbles as we approach Tremont Ave station. Oscar looks at me mischievously, "Hidden treasure, huh? Mind sharing with your buddies?"

I play along, "Depends on how much you help me enjoy my spring break."

We step off the train, the banter continuing as we make our way home. The adventure to the Dominican Republic awaits, filled with the promise of family, discovery, and maybe a touch of treasure.

As we walk out of the subway station onto Tremont Ave, the vibrant rhythm of the Bronx surrounds us. The neighborhood is alive with its unique blend of cultures and personalities.

The local bodega on the corner, its neon sign flickering, beckons us with the promise of snacks and cold drinks. The familiar scent of grilled onions and spices wafts from the street vendors' carts nearby. We decide to stop by the bodega, a tiny but well-stocked place that seems to have everything you could ever need.

Inside, the old wooden floor creaks under our sneakers. The shelves are crammed with an assortment of items, from canned goods to plantains. Behind the counter, the bodega owner, Mr. Rodriguez, nods at us, his eyes never leaving the small TV playing Spanish soap operas in the corner.

As we step back onto the sidewalk, we encounter the iconic scene of the neighborhood. I always see "Doña Carmen" with her red trench coat and is indeed out walking her small white poodle. She gives us a half-smile, her eyes squinting from years of watching over the neighborhood from her apartment window.

Down the block, a group of Jamaican guys played loud reggae music from their car, the bass vibrating through the air. They wave at us, their music turning the street into a lively dance floor.

Crazy Pedro, a regular character in the neighborhood, approaches us with his usual enthusiasm. "Hey, amigos! Got a quarter for me today?"

I dig into my pocket and hand him a quarter. He thanks us with a toothy grin and shuffles off down the street.

As we pass by the building, Jose is at it again, diligently cleaning and polishing his red Pontiac. The rhythmic beats of Frankie Ruiz's salsa music set the pace for his meticulous work. He gives us a nod, and we exchange greetings.

The familiar sights and sounds of the neighborhood accompany us as we make our way home. This place, with its vibrant characters and diverse energy, is the backdrop to our everyday lives, and today, it's the starting point of a new adventure.

3

CHAPTER

…HEY, MOM! HAVE YOU SEEN MY TOOTHBRUSH? I CAN'T FIND IT," I yelled from the top of my lungs as we prepared for our trip.

"Well, mijo, check your bag; you packed them, right?". My mom replied in her calm and angelic voice.

It's already 5:30 a.m., and I see my dad sitting in the living room, glancing at his watch every few minutes. He's always been meticulous about time, especially when it comes to family trips. Even though he'd already confirmed with Joe, our usual driver, I could tell he was anxious. Maybe it was the weight of the surprise he'd planned for my graduation, or maybe it was something deeper—something he wasn't telling us.

The flight is not until 11:00 a.m., and it takes only 45 minutes to JFK from the Bronx. My mom picks up the phone and opens her eyes at me. That's my cue to go that the car is downstairs.

Sure enough, I look down the window and see the same beat-up white van from the 80s; I'm bracing myself because I know it always smells funky. I'm glad I didn't eat anything for breakfast.

Joe, the driver, steps out of the van for a quick smoke. He is from Jamaica; you can tell from his accent and dreadlocks. He has been driving my father to the airport as far as I can remember. My dad is the type of guy who always sticks with the first thing he tries and never goes for something new.

"MOM! What you got in here? It weighs more than a body bag. We are only going to be there for two weeks." I complained as I came down the narrow staircase from our apartment on the 4th floor. My mom always packs as if she is going away for a 3-month trip.

As we made our way to the airport, the air thick with the anticipation of a journey about to unfold, my dad leaned into my mom with a gentle whisper that seemed to carry the weight of a thousand unspoken worries.

"Always keep your passports and documents with you," he said, his voice a soft undercurrent to the bustling sounds of the old van.

My mom, a seasoned traveler with a hint of a smile playing on her lips, replied, "I know, Tony. You've told me a thousand times." Her tone held a mixture of fond exasperation and reassurance, a testament to the countless reminders that had become a prelude to every journey we embarked upon.

But my dad, with a father's instinct that transcended the routine, insisted, "I just want to ensure you're all safe." His eyes, a reflection of years spent shouldering the responsibility of safeguarding his family, spoke volumes. It wasn't merely about passports and documents; it was a silent plea for the well-being of those he held dearest.

I couldn't help but think he worried too much, but I was excited to have a week off from school earlier than anyone else. As we approached the airport, my dad turned to Joe, our driver, and reminded him, "Don't forget to pick us up on the 16th; we'll be arriving on the 2:30 p.m. flight." Joe assured him, "I've got it on my calendar, Mr. Costa." With a hint of sarcasm, Joe asked, "Which terminal again?"

My dad replied, "Terminal 8, American. I assume you wrote it down." He refers to American Airlines as his favorite airline every time he travels.

I could sense the anxiety in my dad's voice. Finally, the John F Kennedy International Airport sign came into view as we approached.

As I assisted Joe in unloading the bags from the van, I noticed my dad embracing my mom tightly, a rare display of emotion from him. "I'm glad we're taking this trip together; it'll be a great opportunity for some quality family time," my mom said.

My dad called out, "Hurry up, Tony! You need to weigh the bags."

I replied, "I know, I know. It's only 6:15 a.m.; we still have three hours." As my mom and I walked towards the check-in counter, my dad rushed back to the van with Joe, probably due to parking officers giving them a hard time for being a non-taxi.

As we waited at the counter to check our bags, I noticed a McDonald's near our gate, and I was starving.

"Mom, we have to walk to gate 3. Can I get McDonald's?" I asked in my most persuasive tone, knowing my mom wouldn't say no. "Please, mom. You know how much I wouldn't say I like plane food, and it's a four-hour flight," I added, trying to make my case for McDonald's.

"Ok, Tony, let's get el jodio Macdonal ese," referring to it with disgust.

4

CHAPTER

After enduring a seemingly interminable two-and-a-half hours of waiting, the sweet relief of progress finally echoed through the airport terminal. The dulcet tones of the crew at the gate calling for first-class passengers rang out, acting as a siren song for the privileged few. It was our cue, albeit a tad premature, to commence the ritual of joining the line that promised boarding and, hopefully, an end to our protracted wait.

With an optimism that bordered on wishful thinking, we began the pilgrimage toward the designated gate, our footsteps infused with a renewed sense of purpose. The prospect of finding our seats and settling into the airplane's embrace was tantalizingly close. Little did we know, a quirky twist awaited us in this prelude to departure.

As we neared the forming line, a subtle disruption unfolded. An old lady, seemingly spry despite her advanced age, navigated her way expertly to the forefront, effortlessly positioning herself ahead of us. A momentary glance between us conveyed a shared sentiment of disbelief, the unspoken question lingering in the air—what just happened?

In response, my mom, with a wry smile adorning her face, met my incredulous gaze. She was no stranger to the unwritten rules of navigating crowded spaces, especially when an old Dominican lady was involved. In that smile, I read an entire chapter of cultural wisdom— a recognition that challenging the precedence of an elder, especially one with a certain Dominican matriarchal aura, was akin to breaching an unspoken code.

The old lady, oblivious to the micro-drama unfolding behind her, continued her confident march toward the gate, a trailblazer in the line formation. And so, we fell in step behind her, our bemusement overshadowed by the shared acknowledgment that some battles were best left unfought.

In those fleeting moments, the airport terminal became a stage for a cultural dance, a ballet of unspoken etiquettes and understandings. My mom's smile served as a gentle reminder that, in the grand tapestry of Dominican social dynamics, the hierarchy of age and respect was a force not to be reckoned with. The old lady, unknowingly, became the matriarch of our impromptu boarding queue.

"Finally, we're in seats 14A and 14B, mom. I got the window seat," I said as I walked down the plane aisle. I always tried to get the window seat, hoping no one would sit next to us. "Attention, passengers, this is a full flight. Please remove your jackets and small bags from the overhead compartments," announced the flight crew. My heart sank as I heard the announcement. "Please, God, not him," I whispered to my mom as I spotted a large man scanning the seats for an empty one. I knew my mom would make me switch seats. Sure enough, I ended up sandwiched between my mom and the man. I could hear every breath he took; it would be a long flight.

After 3 hours, I asked my mom if we could switch seats. I know we are about to land; the captain announced, "Cabin crew, please take your seats for landing." I can see the water already is so beautiful. As the airplane descends, the lush green landscape of The Dominican Republic comes into view.

The deep blue waters of the Caribbean Sea and the Atlantic Ocean glow in the sun, contrasting beautifully with the sandy beaches and swaying palm trees. The coastline is dotted with resorts, and you can see boats and ships moving in the waters. The clear blue sky and the sun shining on the island give a warm welcome. As the plane gets closer to the airport, you can see the bustling city and the mountainous terrain in the distance, giving a sense of adventure awaits you.

As we descended toward Santo Domingo, I couldn't help but feel a sense of excitement. After a long flight, we were finally going to be able to stretch our legs and explore the city. As the plane touches down, a sound of relief and applause can be heard from most passengers. I remember asking my mom why everyone was clapping.

"Bienvenidos al Aeropuerto Internacional de Las Américas en Santo Domingo la hora local es 1:30 p.m." Says the lady from the flight crew. You can hear the sound of people unbuckling before the plane even stops at the gate.

The sound of the seatbelt sign bell ringing filled the cabin as everyone scrambled to grab their bags from the overhead compartments and rush off the plane. However, the doors were not yet open. Passengers were jostling for position, trying to be the first ones off the plane. I saw my mom take a deep breath and remind me to stay calm and not to get caught up in the chaos. As soon as the doors opened, we made our way out of the plane and into the airport. The warm Caribbean air hit my face, and I couldn't help but smile. We had arrived in Santo Domingo, and our adventure was just beginning.

26

As I step off the plane, my heart races with excitement as the vibrant rhythms of the "GTA" Güira, Tambora, and Accordion fill my ears. My mother and I make our way towards immigration control, where the scintillating sounds of the "Perico Ripao" and the alluring aroma of Brugal, the renowned Dominican rum, greet us with open arms. The island nation's energy pulses through my veins, drawing me deeper into its vibrant culture and captivating spirit.

5

CHAPTER

It was a joyful day at the beach in Juan Dolio, the perfect day for a vacation. The sky was a bright blue with no clouds, and the sun shone brightly. Juan Dolio Beach is a stunning stretch of white sand located just 45 minutes east of Santo Domingo. The beach stretches for miles, allowing visitors to spread and soak up the sun.

I can feel the soft and powdery sand between my toes, perfect for playing and lounging. The water is a mesmerizing turquoise color, inviting me to take a dip in the gentle waves. The calm and transparent sea makes it perfect for swimming, snorkeling, and other water activities. The beach is surrounded by lush greenery, adding to the tropical paradise feel of the place. It's the perfect spot to relax, unwind, and enjoy the natural beauty of the Caribbean. With its clear waters and white sandy beach, Juan Dolio is a true Caribbean paradise.

However, amidst the serene tableau of sea and sand, I couldn't shake the feeling that something weighed heavily on my mother's mind.

Seated on a weathered piece of driftwood, she reached into the depths of her beach bag and retrieved her old Nokia phone, its ringtone breaking the gentle symphony of the ocean. The caller ID revealed a truth that shifted the atmosphere. The lines etching worry on her face seemed to deepen as she listened intently.

I couldn't help but voice the concern that hung in the salty breeze, "It's Dad, isn't it?" The words lingered, the gravity of the situation suspended between us like the salty air.

Her gaze met mine, a flicker of acknowledgment in her eyes. The call ended, and in that pregnant pause, I witnessed the transformation. The concern that had furrowed her brow was replaced by an emotional storm, tears welling up as she clutched the phone.

The beach, a canvas of tranquility, became an unwitting witness to our family's unexpected turn of events. As if bracing for the impact of shared sorrow, we found a secluded spot where the sand met the surf. The phone, a tangible link to the news that had disrupted our idyllic day, slipped from her grasp, landing softly on the sun-warmed sand. The waves, once soothing, now seemed to echo the chaos in our hearts.

With a voice that trembled with both grief and determination, she confirmed my unspoken fears, "Yes, it's your father. The ocean's melody seemed to fade, leaving only the distant murmur of the waves and the raw vulnerability that remained in the air.

"He's been in an accident," she whispered, the words carrying the weight of a sudden storm that had disrupted the tranquil beachscape. At that moment, the beach transformed into more than a scenic backdrop; it became the stage for a shared narrative of worry, love, and uncertainty.

We quickly left for New York and headed straight to the Columbia Presbyterian Hospital upon arriving. My heart was pounding with fear as I worried about the severity of my father's condition. I couldn't believe this was happening.

6

CHAPTER

Sitting at his childhood home apartment in the Bronx's dimly lit living room, Tony stares blankly at the envelope in his hands. His mother sat across from him, tears streaming down her face as she tried to compose herself.

"Tony, your father's death... it wasn't an accident," she said, trembling.

Tony's heart sank. He had always suspected there was more to his father's death than the official story, but he never expected to hear these words from his mother. "What do you mean?" he asked, his voice barely above a whisper.

"I don't know all the details, but your father was looking into something related to your grandfather's past business before he died. I think he must have uncovered something, or someone, that put him in danger," his mother replied, her voice cracking with emotion.

Tony's mind raced with a million questions. "Why didn't you tell me this before? Why did you let me believe it was an accident?"

"I didn't want to burden you with this. I thought it was better for you to remember your father as a loving and devoted man, and I'm scared for you. I don't want anything to happen to us," she said, her voice heavy with sorrow.

Tony couldn't believe what he was hearing. His father, the man he had idolized his whole life, had kept secrets from him.

He felt a sense of betrayal wash over him. "Do you know who was behind his death?" he asked, his voice laced with anger.

"I'm not sure. Your father never talked to me about his work; all his documents and files were missing after he died. I think someone must have taken them," his mother replied, her voice barely above a whisper.

Tony knew that he had to find out the truth. He couldn't let his father's death go unsolved. "I'm going to find out what happened. I'll leave no stone unturned," he said, determination in his voice.

"Tony, please be careful. I don't want to lose you too," his mother said, fear in her eyes.

"I will be, I promise," he said, leaning over to hug his mother.

The phone rang; Tony walked to the kitchen and sat, answered with a groggy "Hello?"

"Tony, it's Enzo. I have some bad news," Enzo's voice on the other end of the line was heavy. "Your father's death was no accident."

Enzo is Tony's godfather and the Director of Italian Business Development for the Italian embassy in the Dominican Republic.

Tony sat up straight and opened his eyes wide. "What? How?"

"It's being called an accident, but I think there may be more to the story," Enzo said. "Your father had been investigating information about your grandfather's mine exploration dealings in the past."

Tony's mind was racing. "I don't understand. Why would he be looking into that?"

"I think he may have uncovered something that someone didn't want him to know," Enzo said. "We need to be careful, Tony. I believe your father's death may not have been an accident. I want you to look for your grandfather's journals; they might hold some answers."

Tony's heart was pounding. "Are you saying someone murdered my father?"

"I can't say for sure," Enzo said. "But we need to tread lightly. I'll do my best to find out what happened and keep you updated. And I think those journals may give you the answers you are looking for."

Tony felt a determination rise in him. "I will find those journals, and I won't rest until I find out the truth about my father's death."

"I understand," Enzo said. "Just be careful, Tony. We don't know whom we can trust."

"I will. Thank you, Enzo," Tony said. "I'll talk to you soon."

"Stay safe, Tony," Enzo said before hanging up.

Tony sat on the kitchen table, the weight of the news settling over him like a heavy fog. The room, once familiar and comforting, now felt tinged with an unfamiliar sense of emptiness. His father, a constant presence in his life, was gone, leaving behind an echoing void that seemed to reverberate within the walls.

His mother, sensing the storm of emotions that churned within her son, entered the kitchen quietly. The air was thick with unspoken grief, and as she took a seat beside him, the silence hung between them like a fragile bridge between shared sorrow.

"Tony," she began, her voice a gentle murmur that sought to navigate the delicate terrain of loss. "I know this is incredibly difficult for you. Losing your father—it's unimaginable."

Tony looked at his mother, his eyes a mirror reflecting the turmoil within. "Yeah," he replied, his voice carrying the weight of a reality he was still grappling to accept. "I never thought... I mean, he was always there."

A heavy pause lingered, filled only by the distant sounds of the outside world filtering through the window—the muffled laughter of neighbors, the rhythmic lull of the wind against the curtains.

His mother, her gaze filled with a mixture of empathy and sorrow, reached out to gently squeeze his hand. "We'll get through this, Tony. Together. Your father would want us to be strong."

Tony nodded, a silent acknowledgment of the shared resolve to weather the storm ahead. As his mother spoke, a spark of determination ignited within him. He looked at her, the weight of grief momentarily eclipsed by a glint of purpose in his eyes.

"But, Mom," he began, his voice steadier now, "I can't just accept this without knowing the truth. I need to understand what happened. Dad deserved that much."

His mother, understanding the resolve in her son's voice, nodded in agreement. "We'll find the answers, Tony. Your grandfather's journals—they might hold the key. We owe it to him to know the truth."

Tony took a deep breath, the commitment to unravel the mystery of his father's death taking root. "I'm going to go through Grandpa's journals, Mom. There has to be something there—some clue about what happened."

His mother offered a small, supportive smile. "We'll do it together. Whatever it takes to find the truth, we'll do it together."

And in that shared moment of grief and determination, the bond between mother and son became a silent pact—a promise to seek the truth, not just for themselves but for the man who was now a presence in memories and journals. The room, once cloaked in the heaviness of loss, became a space infused with a shared determination to uncover the answers that lay buried in the pages of a grandfather's journals.

As he left his childhood apartment and stepped out into the bustling streets of the Bronx along Clay Ave, Tony knew that his quest for the truth would be challenging. Still, he was determined to uncover the secrets of his father's past and finally find closure for his family's tragedy.

7

CHAPTER

Tony walked up to the block of 176th Street and tapped Oscar's window on the first floor. "Oscar! Open up!" Tony called out.

Oscar opened the window shades and signaled for Tony to enter the apartment.

Once inside, Tony and Oscar decided to call their friend Luis to join them. Oscar and Tony gathered around the living room table to call Luis. "Hey Luis, sorry to call you so late, but I just found out something important," Tony said.

"What is it?" Luis asked, concerned.

"I just got a call from my godfather Enzo. He told me that my father's death might not have been an accident," Tony said, his voice shaking.

"What? What do you mean?" Oscar asked, shocked.

"He thinks my father may have uncovered something that someone didn't want him to know," Tony explained. "That's why we need to go to my father's office at Columbia University and see what we can find."

"Okay, I'm in," Luis said. "Let's do this and find out the truth about your father's death."

"Yeah, let's do it," Oscar added, determined.

The trio decided to go to Tony's father's office at Columbia University to see what they could find to unravel the truth about Tony's father's death.

In the middle of the cloudy night, the three friends met at 116th Street and Broadway to enter the Columbia University campus. "Are we sure this is a good idea?" Luis asked, his voice shaking with fear.

"We have to do this, Luis," Tony replied. "I need to know the truth."

"Okay, but we need to be careful," Oscar added. "We don't want to get caught."

As they walked towards Schermerhorn Hall, where Tony's father's office was, they evaded two security guards, who almost caught them. "We need to be quick," Oscar said, looking around nervously.

But amid the adrenaline rush, Luis got scared and left. "I can't do this, guys. I don't want to get caught," he said before turning and running away.

"Luis, wait!" Tony called out, but it was too late. Oscar and Tony found themselves under an open window near the Geology department. "Okay, I'll go in, and you keep watch," Tony said.

"Be careful," Oscar replied as he watched while Tony entered the building. Tony found his way to his father's office, the nameplate on the door gleaming under the dim hallway light: *Office of Dean of Geology, Dr. Mario Costa*. His heart pounded as he turned the doorknob, half-expecting an alarm to sound. Inside, the room smelled of old paper and coffee, a familiar scent that brought a pang of grief. He rifled through the files, his hands trembling, until he found a folder labeled *Dominican Republic Mine*. Just as he tucked it into his bag, the sound of footsteps echoed down the hall. He froze, holding his breath, until the guard passed by.

As Oscar stood outside, keeping an eye on the building, a security guard approached him. "Can I help you, sir?" the guard asked, looking at Oscar suspiciously.

Oscar's heart began to race as he thought quickly for a story. "Oh, I'm just waiting for my friend," Oscar said, trying to sound casual. "He's meeting me here to help me with a school project."

The guard looked skeptical. "What kind of project?" he asked.

"It's a geology project," Oscar said, thinking fast. "We're studying the area's different types of rocks and stuff. We're supposed to collect samples and do some analysis of them."

The guard nodded, still looking skeptical. "I see. And where is your friend now?"

"He's just inside, getting some samples," Oscar said, pointing to the building. "He should be out any minute now."

The guard looked at the building and then back at Oscar. "Okay, be sure to stay out of any restricted areas. And be sure to have your ID ready if we need to check."

"Of course, of course," Oscar said, nodding quickly. "We'll be sure to do that."

The guard gave him one more suspicious look before turning and walking away. Oscar let out a sigh of relief and waited for Tony to return safely. He was glad he could think on his feet and create a story that convinced the security guard to leave him alone.

As Tony searched through the files in his father's office, his heart was pounding with anticipation. He knew that he was getting close to uncovering the truth about his father's death. Finally, his eyes fell on a folder labeled "Dominican Republic Mine." He knew that this was it.

Tony quickly opened the folder and began reading through the contents. Inside, he found information about a mine in the Dominican Republic that his father had been researching. There were maps, geological reports, and notes scribbled in his father's handwriting.

Tony couldn't believe what he was reading. His father had uncovered something big that someone didn't want him to know. As he read through the reports, he realized that his father had found a massive deposit of gold and other precious minerals at the mine.

As he read further, Tony found a set of keys with an address. He knew that this was it. This was the key to uncovering the truth about his father's death. He quickly put the keys and the folder in his backpack and signaled Oscar to leave.

Tony's thoughts were racing as he left the building. He couldn't believe what he had found. His father had uncovered something big that someone didn't want him to know. He was determined to uncover the truth, no matter what it took. He knew this was the starting point of a long journey, but he was ready for it.

Tony and Oscar were just about to leave the building when they heard a loud voice behind them. "Hey, you! Stop right there!" It was a security guard. They knew they had been caught.

Tony and Oscar started running, but the guard was quick on their heels. They darted through the halls, trying to find a way out. Finally, they made it to the exit and burst through the doors.

The night air was cool and crisp, but Tony and Oscar were sweating and out of breath. They sprinted across the lawn, hoping to lose the guard in the darkness. But he was still on their tail, shouting into his radio for backup.

Tony and Oscar turned a corner and found themselves at a dead end. They were trapped. The guard caught up to them, panting and red-faced. "All right, you two. Give me that envelope you took from the office," he demanded.

Tony hesitated, but he knew that he had no choice. He handed the envelope, and the guard snatched it from his hand. But as the guard checked the envelope contents, Tony remembered the keys with the address on the keychain he had slipped into his backpack.

"Okay, you two. You're under arrest for breaking," the guard said as he led them back to the building.

Tony's heart sank as he realized what he had done. He had been caught, and the truth about his father's death would remain hidden. As they were taken to the security office, Tony's thoughts were jumbled. He couldn't believe this was happening.

As the security guard led Tony and Oscar back to the security office, Oscar subtly gestured toward the exit. Tony knew exactly what he meant. They had to make a run for it.

Without warning, Tony and Oscar bolted for the exit. They ran like lightning. They reached the door, and Tony yanked it open, pulling Oscar with him. They burst into the night air and took off running.

The security guards were caught off guard, but they quickly gave chase. Tony and Oscar sprinted across the lawn, their hearts pounding in their chest. They could hear the guards behind them shouting into their radios for backup.

Tony and Oscar reached the street and kept running. They could see the subway station in the distance, and they knew that was their only hope of escape. They ran like their lives depended on it, their feet pounding the pavement.

They reached the subway station, and without breaking stride, they charged down the steps. They got to the platform and jumped onto the first train that had arrived. As the train pulled away from the station, they both collapsed on the seats, panting and out of breath.

Oscar looked at Tony with a face of defeat. "We lost the envelope," Oscar said, the disappointment evident in his voice. "All that work, and we don't even have the proof we need."

Tony smiled and reached into his backpack. "Don't be so sure," he said, pulling out the keys he had taken from his father's office. "I kept these in my backpack; I wasn't going to let them get caught."

Oscar's eyes widened in surprise. "You kept the keys? Tony, you're a genius!"

Tony grinned. "I knew they were important. I couldn't risk losing them. With these keys, we can finally get to the bottom of what happened to my father."

On one side, the address read "230 230W ST, BX, NY." On the other the number "1812."

Oscar nodded. "And the address on the keychain, that's probably where we'll find the answers we need."

Tony nodded. "Exactly. We're not done yet. We still have a long way to go, but we're one step closer to the truth."

Oscar smiled. "Let's go then. We don't have a moment to lose."

Tony and Oscar stood up, ready to continue their journey to uncover the truth about Tony's father's death. They knew that it wouldn't be easy, but they were determined to get to the bottom of it, no matter what it took.

They both knew this was not the end of the chase but a temporary escape. They were both excited about their discovery but worried about what it could mean. They had uncovered a piece of the puzzle in uncovering the truth about Tony's father's death, but they knew there was still a long way to go.

8

CHAPTER

Tony woke up early the next day, his mind racing with thoughts of the keys he had taken from his father's office. He knew he needed to find out where the keychain address led, and Oscar could help him.

Tony caught up with Oscar at his house. "I've been thinking about the keys we found last night," Tony said. "I think I know where they might lead us."

"Where?" Oscar asked.

"The address on the keychain, it's a U-Haul storage at 230th Street," Tony replied. "I think that's where we'll find the answers we're looking for."

Oscar nodded. "All right, let's go check it out."

Tony and Oscar arrived at the U-Haul location at 230th Street in the Bronx. Tony and Oscar exchanged glances, their shared curiosity etched on their faces as they ventured into the storage building.

With a swift turn of the key, they opened the metal door to storage bin 1812, revealing a world that seemed frozen in time. Dust particles danced in the air as the door creaked open, unveiling a trove of forgotten artifacts and the echoes of a bygone era.

Tony's eyes widened as they fell upon a collection of laboratory containers neatly arranged on shelves—a silent testament to a scientific pursuit that once thrived. "Look at this, Oscar," he exclaimed, picking up a beaker and turning it in his hands. "These are old, like really old. Grandpa's lab equipment, I guess."

Oscar, his eyes scanning the array of scientific paraphernalia, grinned. "Man, this is like stepping into a time machine. Your grandpa was serious about his experiments, huh?"

Tony nodded, a mix of nostalgia and fascination playing on his features. "Yeah, he was. I mean, I knew he was into science, but I never thought he had a whole lab's worth of stuff stashed away."

As they delved deeper into the storage unit, they unearthed more treasures—a trove of old books with weathered spines, each one carrying the weight of accumulated knowledge. Tony leafed through one of them, his fingers tracing the faded words. "These must be his research notes or something. I had no idea he kept all this."

Oscar, now examining an ancient microscope with a discerning eye, chimed in, "Your grandpa was no ordinary guy. Looks like he had a whole setup here."

Amidst the scientific relics, they stumbled upon lab furniture, each piece whispering tales of experiments conducted and discoveries made. Tony ran his hand along the edge of a worn wooden table, the surface marked with the scars of a thousand scientific endeavors.

"This is incredible," Tony mused, his voice tinged with awe. "I had no clue he was so into all this. It's like he had a secret life."

Oscar chuckled, "Secret scientist Grandpa. Who would've thought?"

As they continued to explore the storage bin, each discovery fueled their curiosity and added layers to the enigma of Tony's grandfather. The dialogue between them unfolded like a narrative, a journey back in time guided by the remnants of a hidden laboratory—a place where scientific dreams once took flight and where the echoes of discovery lingered in the air.

"It looks like old things from a school lab class," Oscar said as he rummaged through the containers.

Tony nodded. "Yeah, I think you're right."

They searched through the storage bin, but they couldn't find anything that seemed important. Just as they were about to give up, Oscar stumbled upon a file cabinet hidden behind old maps and covered with an old painter's mantle.

"Tony, look at this," Oscar said as he pulled the file cabinet out from behind the maps.

Tony opened the file cabinet and found a set of brown leather-covered books that looked like journals.

On the front of each book were the initials "AR" in large letters. Tony knew right away that these were his grandfather's journals.

"Oscar, look," Tony said, his voice filled with excitement. "These are my grandfather's journals. This is it; this should have the answer.

Tony's hands trembled as he opened the first journal. Inside, he found page after page of meticulous notes and observations, all written in his grandfather's neat handwriting. He flipped through the pages, scanning the words and taking in the information. He was immediately struck by how detailed and thorough his grandfather's notes were.

As Tony read through the journal, he felt a sense of awe and respect for his grandfather. The man had been a true scientist, dedicated to his work and passionate about his research.

The entries particularly struck Tony about the mine in the Dominican Republic. His grandfather had written about the mine's history, the challenges he and his team had faced, and the discoveries they had made.

He also wrote about the time's political and social context and how it affected their work.

Tony felt a sense of pride and connection to his grandfather as he read through the journal. He realized that his father had been following in his grandfather's footsteps and that his father's death had something to do with the mine and the information his grandfather had uncovered.

Tony knew that he had to continue reading the journals, to find out more about the mine and to uncover the truth about his father's death. He felt a renewed determination and knew he had to finish what his father and grandfather had started.

Tony and Oscar rushed back to Tony's apartment, eager to read the journals they had found in the storage unit. The day had grown cloudy, and it seemed that it was about to start raining. As they entered the apartment, Tony's mother was sitting in the living room, watching the news on TV.

"Tony, where have you been?" his mother asked.

Tony didn't answer; he rushed past her, heading straight to his room. He closed the door behind him, with Oscar following closely behind. Tony closed the window shades and flicked on the desk light, sitting on his chair and laying the journals on his desk. Oscar sat impatiently on Tony's bed, watching as Tony carefully lifted the first journal from the pile, his hands trembling with anticipation. The journal was bound in a dark brown leather cover, with the initials "AR" embossed in gold on the front. He ran his fingers over the cover, feeling the smooth texture of the old leather and the worn edges of the pages.

Tony flipped open the journal to the first page and began reading. The journal entry was dated June 15, 1942.

Today has been a long and grueling day. We were stationed in Sicily, trying to push back the enemy's advance. The fighting has been intense, and the casualties have been high. I have seen things that I never thought I would have to see in my life. The screams of the wounded and dying, the smell of death in the air, it's all too much to bear.

I have lost many of my comrades today, men I had grown close to over the months we have been stationed here. I can't help but wonder if I will be next. The thought of dying here, so far from home, is a constant weight on my mind.

I often think of my home and my people and pray they are safe. I fear for their safety, as the enemy seems to be getting closer and closer to our shores. I wish I could be there to protect them, but I am here, fighting a war that I am not sure I believe in anymore.

I have seen the atrocities committed by both sides, and I can no longer justify the violence and destruction. I have realized that this war is not about freedom and justice but power and greed.

I do not know what the future holds, but I fear for the fate of my country. I can only hope that this war will end one day and that we can begin to rebuild and heal from the wounds inflicted upon us.

During the spring of 1943, Sicily was under Nazi Occupation. Despite the oppression and harsh living conditions, the Italians showed little resistance. However, as the Allied forces began progressing, the Italians joined forces with them. Before the landings, Sicily was one of the worst-affected regions in Italy, with food rationing and a thriving black market due to an air and naval blockade. The Allies heavily bombed the island, causing widespread destruction and making it difficult for locals to find shelter. Many sought refuges in stables, caves, and grottoes; in Ortygia, they even took to the tunnel complex under the cathedral. In Catania, they hid in the tunnels of the Roman amphitheater, desperate to escape the relentless bombing.

Antonio's comrades were hungry and desperate for something to eat. They turned to Antonio, knowing he had a knack for finding food in the most unlikely places.

"Antonio, can you go out and see if you can find something for us to eat? Preferably not your boot because we've had enough of that," one of his comrades, Marco, asked him jokingly.

"I'll do my best, but I can't make any promises. I'll see if I can find something better than my boot," Antonio replied with a chuckle, feeling the weight of responsibility on his shoulders.

He set out into the war-torn streets, searching for any sign of food. But the roads were empty, the shops were closed, and the markets were barren. Antonio searched high and low but could only find a few rats scurrying around in the alleys.

As Antonio walked through the deserted streets, he couldn't shake off the feeling of defeat. He had searched every corner, every alley, and every shop, but all he could find were closed doors and empty shelves. He was about to give up when he heard the faint sound of scurrying coming from an alleyway. He cautiously made his way toward the sound and saw a group of rats running around. At first, he was disgusted by the thought of eating rats, but as the hunger pains grew stronger, he realized that this might be their only option.

He quickly scanned the alley for something to catch the rats with; his eyes landed on a nearby trash can lid. He lifted it, and with a swift motion, he trapped one of the rats beneath it. He repeated the process until he had caught three rats, he felt a mix of guilt and regret for having to resort to such measures, but he knew it was necessary to keep himself and his comrades alive.

As he walked back to the barracks, he couldn't help but think about the harsh realities of war and how it had reduced him to catching rats for food. He thought about his family back home and how they were probably struggling just as much as he was. He made a silent promise to himself that once the war was over, he would never let himself or his loved ones go hungry again.

Antonio made his way back to the barracks. His comrades were waiting anxiously for his return.

"Did you find anything? Or are you going to make us eat your socks again?" asked Marco.

"I Did; I found something better than my boot or socks; I found some pigeons," Antonio lied smoothly, trying to conceal the truth.

His comrades were excited at the prospect of a proper meal and thanked Antonio for his efforts. As they sat down to eat, Antonio couldn't help but feel a twinge of guilt for not disclosing the true origins of their meal. But he rationalized that it was for the greater good, and his comrades needed to eat. The meal was a success, and they all enjoyed it, and Antonio was relieved that his secret was safe.

9

CHAPTER

August 10th, 1943

It has been a long and grueling day. The Americans and allied forces have taken over most of Sicily. The Italian Fascist Grand Council passed a vote of no confidence on Mussolini, and it was clear that he had no power over us anymore. This is a lost war.

I'm not sure what I am doing here. I joined the army to serve my country, but now it seems like I am fighting a losing battle. I have seen so much death and destruction; it is hard to see any purpose in it all.

Antonio was on the front lines of the battle for Sicily. The American and Allied forces were making their way through the island, and the Axis powers were in retreat. Antonio and his comrades were caught in the middle of the gunfire, trying to stay alive as long as they could.

"Come on, Antonio! We have to keep moving!" shouted Giuseppe, one of Antonio's closest friends in the unit.

"I'm doing my best, Giuseppe!" Antonio shouted back, trying to keep up with his friend as they ran through the streets.

The sound of gunfire and explosions filled the air, and Antonio could feel the fear and adrenaline pumping through his veins. He knew that he could be hit by a bullet or a piece of shrapnel at any moment.

"This is it; we're done for!" Marco shouted.

"Don't give up yet; we still have a chance!" Antonio yelled back, determined to survive.

But then, a bullet found its way through Antonio's leg, and he fell to the ground in pain. He could hear his friends calling out to him, but everything was becoming a blur. He thought to himself, "I'm not sure what I am doing here. This war is lost, and I may not make it out alive."

Despite the pain and agony, Antonio managed to drag himself to safety and escape from Sicily. He knew he was lucky to be alive, and he couldn't help but regret being caught up in the middle of such a brutal conflict.

As Antonio lay on the ground, he knew he had to find a way to escape Sicily. He gritted his teeth against the pain in his leg, and with a determined effort, he dragged himself to his feet. He could hear the gunfire getting closer and closer, and he knew he had to move quickly.

"Marco, Giuseppe, I need your help," Antonio called out to his friends.

"What can we do, Antonio?" asked Marco as he and Giuseppe rushed over to him.

"We need to get out of here and fast. I have an idea, but I need you to trust me," Antonio said, his voice strained with pain.

Without hesitation, Marco and Giuseppe helped Antonio hobble toward the edge of town. They saw a small boat tied up at the shore and saw their chance.

They untied the boat and helped Antonio on board.

"We need to get away from here, as far as we can," Antonio said as they pushed off from the shore.

"Where are we going?" asked Giuseppe as they set sail.

"Rome, my sister's house, she will help us," Antonio replied.

The journey was not easy; they had to avoid enemy patrols and navigate through dangerous waters, but eventually, they made it to Rome.

Antonio limped up to his sister Etna's front door in Rome. He had managed to escape from Sicily with the help of his fellow soldiers. His leg was bleeding, and he was weak from the long journey.

As he knocked on the door, he could hear Etna's footsteps approaching. She opened the door and immediately recognized her brother. "Antonio! What happened? Are you okay?" she exclaimed; her voice full of concern.

"I'm fine, just a bullet wound on my leg. I need your help," Antonio replied, leaning on his sister for support as he hobbled inside.

Etna quickly helped him to the couch and fetched some water and a first aid kit. "Let me take a look at your leg," she said as she gently examined the wound. "It's not too deep, but it needs to be cleaned and dressed."

As Etna tended to his wound, Antonio explained to her what had happened in Sicily. "It's a lost war," he said, "I don't know what I was doing there. I just had to fire shots to stay alive as long as I could."

Etna listened with a heavy heart, understanding the gravity of the situation. "We need to get you out of here," she said, "I know some people who can help us. We'll get you a new identity and a way out of the country."

As Etna worked on arranging for his escape, Antonio spent the next few weeks recovering at her house. They talked about their family and their plans for the future.

"I can't thank you enough, Etna," Antonio said one day as they sat together in the living room.

"You're my brother," Etna replied with a smile, "I'll always be here for you."

10

CHAPTER

My brother Mario wrote to me on October 15th, 1952, his handwriting neat but hurried, as if he couldn't wait to share his thoughts. "My dear brother," he began, "I cannot express the excitement I feel about the possibilities in this new world. The history of mining in the Caribbean is rich, and I truly believe that there is still so much left to discover. The Spanish may have abandoned these mines centuries ago, but I sense there's gold—and perhaps more—waiting for us. I would be honored if you would join me in this endeavor, and together we can uncover the secrets of the past and build a better future for ourselves."

My brother Mario Rossi is a graduate geologist passionate about the stories and fables of the new world. He had always been fascinated with the history of mine exploration and the potential for discovery in the Caribbean.

During his studies in Spain, Mario came across a book from the 1500s about the Spanish's exploitation of gold deposits in Hispaniola. He became captivated by the idea of uncovering these lost mines and their potential wealth.

Mario learned about how in the 1500s, the king of Spain sent Don Juan Nieto and Balcárcel to Hispaniola to explore gold deposits; he informed about a mine in a report sent to the ruler, in which he suggested that the exploitation of the deposits should be restored since he said had produced more than one million crowns to the throne annually.

According to old documents, Spain began exploiting the mine in 1505. After fifteen years, it was abandoned, not due to a shortage of ore but of laborers.

As he delved deeper into his research, Mario realized that the Dominican Republic was one of the most promising places to explore. He began reaching out to local contacts and gathering information about the mining operations in the area, which was none.

Then, he decided to write to his brother Antonio, who was still living in Italy. In his letter, Mario told Antonio about the potential for wealth and adventure in the Dominican Republic and urged him to join him in his exploration efforts.

Antonio was hesitant at first, still recovering from the war and the wounds of Sicily. But the more he thought about it, the more he realized that this could be a lifetime opportunity.

Finally, Tony closed the journal and sat back in his chair. He couldn't believe how much he had learned from his grandfather's diary and how much it had affected him. He knew that he would be reading it again and again and that it would always hold a special place in his heart. He felt grateful for this glimpse into his grandfather's life and the understanding it gave him of his family history and the sacrifices made by his grandfather and many others during the war.

11

CHAPTER

July 15th, 1952

Today, I embarked on a journey that I never thought I would have to take. I left my home country of Italy, leaving behind my family and my past. I boarded a merchant boat headed for the Dominican Republic under the guise of a Franciscan monk and a new identity, "Enrique Costa."

The journey was long and grueling, 15 days at sea, but I found solace in the company of a beautiful woman named Isabella. She was on her way to Santo Domingo. We spent most of our days talking, and I couldn't help but find myself falling for her. She had a contagious laughter and a spark in her eyes that I couldn't resist.

We shared many laughs and even some dances on deck under the stars. She taught me a few salsa moves that will come in handy when I finally arrive in the Caribbean.

As much as I enjoyed Isabella's company, I could not shake off the dread lingering in my mind. I am not just traveling to a new place; I am running away from my past. But I must keep my mind on finding the abandoned mine my brother Mario and cousin Pablo are searching for.

I am unsure of the future, but I am ready to face it head-on.

Until next time,

Enrique "kike" Costa.

12

CHAPTER

In the summer of 1952, Antonio Rossi defected from his country, leaving his family behind for a better future in the new world. He knew the war in Europe was not going well for the Axis powers, and he would be prosecuted sooner or later.

It was a bright and sunny day as I boarded the merchant ship in the port of Livorno. The sea was calm, and the sky was a clear blue. I was dressed as a Franciscan monk, my new identity Enrique Costa, and carrying only a small satchel with a few essentials. I felt mixed emotions as I boarded the merchant boat that would take me on a 15-day journey to the Dominican Republic.

As I settled into my cabin, I couldn't help but feel a sense of excitement and uncertainty. I was leaving behind everything I knew and embarking on a new adventure to reunite with my brother Mario and cousin Pablo.

As the days passed, I found myself growing increasingly restless. The ship was packed with other passengers, but most kept them to themselves.

But my journey was not without its surprises. On the second day, I met a young woman named Isabella. She was fiery and adventurous, always eager to explore the ship and start a conversation. Despite my disguise as a monk, I was drawn to her, and we spent many hours talking and laughing together.

Isabella was dressed in formal, elegant attire, and her hair was styled in a fashionable updo. She had an air of wealth and class about her. She had inherited a large sum of money from her deceased husband. She was on her way to the Caribbean to escape the memories of her loss and start anew.

Isabella had a great sense of humor and always found a way to make me laugh, even when I was feeling homesick.

"I can't believe you're traveling to the Caribbean dressed as a monk," Isabella said with a chuckle as we sat on the deck.

"Well, it's a long story," Antonio replied, trying to keep his cover.

"I've got time," she said with a smile.

She was kind, funny, and had a contagious energy. I told her more and more about myself, even though I was supposed to keep a low profile.

"I'm going to the Dominican Republic to reunite with my brother," he told her one day.

"Really? What does he do there?" she asked.

"He's a geologist," Antonio replied. "He's been there for years, searching for a lost mine."

Isabella's eyes widened. "A lost mine? That sounds like an adventure."

"It is," Antonio said with a smile. "I just hope I can find it."

One night, as the boat sailed through the Caribbean Sea, a fierce storm hit. The waves grew higher and higher, and the winds howled. The crew fought to keep the ship afloat, but it was clear that they were in grave danger.

Suddenly, a storm rolled in, and the waves grew choppy. The boat began to rock violently, and the crew rushed to secure the deck. In the chaos, Isabella lost her footing and fell overboard. Antonio quickly jumped in after her, but the current was strong, and they were pulled away from the boat.

The crew threw out a life raft and managed to rescue them both, but not before they were caught in a riptide and pulled out to sea. As the storm raged, Antonio and Isabella's spirits began to falter. They were cold, wet, and exhausted, and they knew their chances of survival were slim. But they didn't give up hope. They kept each other's spirits up, knowing that they needed to be strong for one another.

They were lost for hours, drifting on the life raft until they were finally rescued by a passing fishing boat. The experience shook Isabella, and Antonio felt guilty for getting her into trouble.

13

CHAPTER

As the boat approached the island's shore, Antonio couldn't help but feel a sense of excitement and nervousness wash over him. He had been on this journey for 15 days, and the end was finally in sight. He walked out onto the deck, taking in the fresh sea air and the warm sun on his face. As he looked out over the horizon, he saw the lights of Santo Domingo twinkling in the distance.

Isabella walked up beside him. She looked over the island with him and said, "It's beautiful, isn't it? I've never been to the Caribbean before. I can't wait to see what it's like."

Antonio smiled at her and replied, "It's breathtaking. I haven't been to the Caribbean either. I'm excited to see what it has to offer."

As the boat drew closer to the shore, the lights of Santo Domingo grew brighter. The city was alive with energy, and Antonio couldn't wait to set foot on the island and start his new life. He turned to Isabella and said, "Are you ready for this?"

She grinned and nodded, "I'm ready for anything."

And with that, the boat finally docked in Santo Domingo, and it was time for him to say goodbye to Isabella.

"I wish you the best of luck in your search," she said as they hugged goodbye.

"Thank you," Antonio replied. "I'll never forget our time on this boat."

As the days passed, I found myself becoming more and more excited for the opportunity that lay ahead. I knew it would not be easy, but I was determined to make the most of it. I couldn't wait to be reunited with my brother and cousin and begin the search for the abandoned mine that had captivated Mario's imagination for so long.

Antonio finally arrived in Santo Domingo. Disembarking from the ship, he made his way to the port exit and was greeted by a group of men. One of them, a tall, balding man with a thick mustache, stepped forward and said, "Welcome to the Dominican Republic, my brother."

Antonio was overjoyed to see his brother and the two men hugged tightly. "I can't believe it, Mario! I never thought I would see you again," Antonio said, tears streaming down his face.

"I'm so glad you made it, brother," Mario replied. "We have much to catch up on. But first, let me introduce you to our cousin Pablo. He's a geologist, and he's been working with the expedition."

Pablo stepped forward and shook Antonio's hand. "Welcome, Antonio. Do you remember me?" asked Pablo with a huge smile.

"Call me Enrique.", said Antonio with a big smile.

"Enrique?" Pablo asked, confused.

"Yes," Mario said with a chuckle. "We had to give him a new identity. The Dominican Republic is under the dictatorship of Rafael Trujillo, and we can't risk him being discovered as a defector. From now on, he will be known as Enrique Costa, Kike."

Antonio nodded, understanding the importance of keeping a low profile. "I'll do whatever it takes to stay safe and help you with your expedition," he said.

That day I understood that my life was turning for good and new adventures were ahead of me. This Island was going to bring the best of me. I went with them to an old cantina on the Malecon for much-needed drinks.

14

CHAPTER

Mario took us to El Vesuvio an enchanting Italian restaurant perched along the Malecón. The ambiance was sophisticated, with a backdrop of the Caribbean Sea stretching out into the horizon. Mario led them to a table strategically placed to capture the breathtaking view, a privilege afforded by his friend's ownership of the establishment.

Seated at the table, the trio took in the panorama of the sea, the waves whispering tales of distant adventures. Mario, positioned at the head of the table, reached for an old, leather-bound book that seemed to hold the secrets of centuries past. He opened it with a certain reverence, the pages crackling softly as if awakening from a long slumber.

Pablo, eyeing the book with curiosity, couldn't help but ask, "What's that, Mario? Some ancient treasure map?"

Mario chuckled, "Not a map, Pablo, but something equally valuable. This," he gestured to the book spread before him, "is where it all began. My fascination with the gold mine started here."

As he began to flip through the pages, the air filled with the scent of history and adventure. Kike, his interest piqued, leaned forward, asking, "How did you end up reading ancient Spanish explorer books?"

Mario grinned, "Back in college, I stumbled upon these old texts from the 1500s. Stories of Spanish adventurers and explorers who roamed these lands centuries ago. And within these pages, I found hints, clues, and tales of a gold mine that held more secrets than anyone could fathom."

The trio listened intently as Mario's narrative unfolded, his voice carrying the weight of discovery and the thrill of untold stories. "The more I read," he continued, "the more convinced I became that there was still gold waiting to be discovered in that mine. It was just a matter of uncovering the clues hidden within these ancient texts."

Pablo grinned, lifting his glass in a silent toast. "To ancient books and hidden treasures," he proposed.

Kike joined in, "And to Mario, the modern-day explorer."

As the glasses clinked, the trio found themselves at the nexus of history and possibility. The restaurant, overlooking the vast expanse of the Caribbean, became a sanctuary where the dreams of old explorers resonated with the aspirations of those seated at the table. And within the pages of that old, leather-bound book, the promise of a new adventure awaited; one that would take them deep into the heart of a forgotten gold mine and the echoes of centuries past.

As he continued to flip through the pages, Mario's voice grew more animated. "The more I read, the more I became convinced that there was still gold to be found in the mine. It was just a matter of finding it."

After finishing his studies, Mario became obsessed with the idea of finding the lost gold mine. He poured over maps and historical documents, and eventually made his way to the Dominican Republic.

As he began to explore the region, Mario realized that the government was reluctant to allow anyone to search for the mine. But he was determined to persuade them otherwise.

"I told them that the riches we could uncover would be beyond their wildest imagination," he recounted. "I showed them the historical documents and maps I had collected and convinced them that the mine was worth exploring."

After months of negotiations, I finally received permission to explore the remains of the gold mine from the Man itself. Trujillo sent for me and asked me to gather a team of experts, to begin to excavate the site.

On our first day in the mine, we uncover small veins of gold. My heart raced with excitement as I realized that we were on the right track. And that's why you are here my bother. Tomorrow, we take over to the cave I have a good feeling about.

I can't wait I said with excitement. Tomorrow is going to be a great day as we all lift our glasses and cheer with Brugal Rum.

15

CHAPTER

It was the Morning of August 7, 1953, I remember it quite well. Beautiful blue sky and warm breeze we started our trip to Cotuí.

Cotuí is a city in the central region of the Dominican Republic and is one of the oldest cities of the New World. It is the capital of Sánchez Ramírez Province in the Cibao. We headed to the mountains of Pueblo Viejo.

As the team approached the abandoned native Indian cave, they couldn't help but feel a sense of excitement and trepidation. The cave was once a source of gold for the Spanish colonists during the 1500s and had been exploited to the point of exhaustion. However, rumors persisted that there was still gold to be found in the depths of the cave, and the team was determined to find it.

As the team entered the cave, Pablo's voice echoed off the walls, "This place is incredible, can you believe it?"

"I know right," Mario replied, "It's amazing to think about how much history is hidden here."

As they made their way deeper into the cave, the team was struck by the intricate carvings on the walls. It was clear that this cave held great significance for the native Tainos who once inhabited the area.

As they continued to walk, Kike added, "I can't wait to see what else we'll find in here. I hope we discover something truly special."

As they continued their exploration, the team stumbled upon a small opening in the cave wall. Curiosity getting the better of them, they decided to investigate further. To their surprise, they found a small chamber filled with artifacts from the Taino culture.

Pablo's eyes widened with awe as they uncovered the artifacts hidden within the depths of the cave. "Wow! Look at all this. We have to document everything, and make sure we preserve it," he exclaimed, his excitement palpable.

Amidst the dim glow of their flashlights, the team marveled at the intricate details and markings on the Taino artifacts. "It's amazing to see how skilled Taino people were at carving," Mario remarked, a sense of reverence in his voice as he observed the craftsmanship of a particularly delicate piece.

As they continued their exploration, the cave whispered the tales of its history. The remnants of the Taino civilization stood in silent testimony to a bygone era. However, alongside the Taino artifacts, signs of the Spanish colonists' presence became evident. Discarded mining debris and remnants of archaic mining equipment hinted at a tumultuous chapter in the cave's past.

Mario, tracing his fingers along the worn edges of a Taino ceremonial object, couldn't help but express his emotions, "We have discovered so much today. It's important to keep this a secret until we meet with El Jefe," a reference to Trujillo, the Island Dictator.

Pablo nodded knowingly, recognizing the delicate nature of their discovery. "We need to get our story together before we pitch to him what we are trying to do here. We can't let his people know just yet," he advised, emphasizing the need for caution.

As they made their way back to the surface, the weight of their findings hung in the air. The team emerged from the cave with a profound sense of accomplishment. They had not only explored the depths of an abandoned Taino cave but had also unearthed artifacts of great cultural significance, shedding light on the complex history of the region.

Looking back at the cave's entrance, they shared a moment of reflection. The cave held the secrets of a bygone era, and as they prepared to meet with the powerful General, the team understood the importance of the delicate dance between discovery and discretion. Their journey into the heart of the island's history had only just begun.

16

CHAPTER

As we gathered around the table with Ambassador Martinez, I couldn't help but feel a sense of nervous excitement. This man had the ear of El Jefe himself, and his power and influence were not to be underestimated.

"¿Como están eso doctores?" said Mr. Martinez, his voice dripping with arrogance as he took a puff of his cigar. He leaned back in his chair and looked around the room, his eyes lingering on each of us for a moment before settling on Mario.

I studied Martinez as he spoke, taking in his sharp features and confident demeanor. He was a successful businessman, and the owner of several major enterprises in the country, and his relationship with Trujillo was well-known. It was no surprise when he was named head of the Ministry of Mining for the Dominican Republic.

"So, Mario, you seem confident about this expedition," he said, the smirk still firmly in place.

Mario bristled at the tone of Mr. Martinez's voice. "I am confident," he said, his voice low and even. "I've done my research; I know what's out there."

Mario had already spoken to Martinez, and I could see the glint of gold in his eyes as he pulled out samples to show off. He spoke with a passionate intensity, convincing Martinez of the potential riches that lay waiting to be uncovered in Pueblo Viejo.

Martinez leaned back in his chair, considering Mario's proposal. I held my breath, waiting for his response.

Finally, he spoke. "I like what I hear," he said, his voice smooth as silk. "I think we can come up with the investment for the equipment you need."

Mr. Martinez chuckled. "And I've talked to Trujillo himself. He's expecting results, you know."

Mario raised an eyebrow. "I'm not sure I understand."

Mr. Martinez leaned forward, his eyes glittering with malice. "If we don't find what we're looking for, there will be consequences. Severe consequences."

"El Jefe no juega", he said. Meaning that Trujillo doesn't play.

The room fell silent, everyone understanding the threat behind his words.

"Look," Mario said, his voice firm. "I know what's at stake here. I've done my homework; I know the risks. But I believe in what we're doing, and I'm willing to take that risk."

Mr. Martinez snorted. "We'll see how long that confidence lasts," he said, before standing up and walking out of the room, his cigar smoke trailing behind him.

Mario leaned back in his chair, his expression grim. "We need to be careful," he said. "Mr. Martinez is not someone to be taken lightly."

The rest of us nodded our faces set with determination. We knew the risks, but we also knew the potential rewards. We were going to find that gold, no matter what it took. We were one step closer to uncovering the treasure of Pueblo Viejo, and it was all thanks to Mario's persuasive skills and Martinez's connections.

As we wrapped up the meeting and said our goodbyes, I couldn't help but feel a sense of excitement and anticipation. We were embarking on a dangerous journey, but with the support of men like Martinez, we just might succeed.

17

CHAPTER

With Ambassador Martinez's investment secured, our team quickly headed to the town of Cotui with all the equipment we needed. Excitement and anticipation buzzed through the air as we began to set up the dig site at Pueblo Viejo, eager to uncover the riches that lay hidden beneath the earth.

As we delved into the earth, the passage of time transformed days into weeks, and each day brought forth a fresh challenge. The sulfide ores stubbornly clung to their golden secrets, resisting our conventional methods and casting a shadow of frustration over our endeavors. Yet, undeterred, we pressed on with unwavering determination.

In the midst of our collective struggle, Mario, our fearless and ever-optimistic leader, had a moment of revelation. "What if," he proposed with a mischievous glint in his eye, "we try something the old-timers never thought of?"

Pablo chuckled, "Oh, the 'Eureka' moment is upon us. Do enlighten us, Mario."

With an air of theatrical mystery, Mario unveiled his daring plan to extract gold from the sulfide ores—a method that had never graced the shores of the Dominican Republic before. There was a pause, a collective holding of breath, as we weighed the risks and rewards of this uncharted territory.

"We might be onto something big," Mario declared, his optimism infectious.

And so, with a mixture of trepidation and excitement, we set Mario's ingenious plan into motion. The machinery hummed, the earth seemed to hold its breath, and then, as if the universe itself acknowledged the audacity of our venture, it happened—like magic.

The sulfide ores relinquished their grip, and there it was—a glimmering cascade of gold, spilling into the light like liquid sunlight. We stood in awe, the air thick with the scent of earth and metal, as the sunlight caught each particle, turning it into a miniature beacon of success. Mario let out a whoop of triumph, his voice echoing through the cavern, while Pablo crossed himself, murmuring a prayer of thanks.

Enrique couldn't help but crack a smile, "Well, Mario, I guess you can add 'Alchemy' to your resume now."

Mario, basking in the glow of our achievement, winked and replied, "Who knew turning sulfide into gold could be so much fun?"

Laughter echoed through the mining site, a jubilant symphony that drowned out the echoes of earlier frustrations. Our journey through the subterranean realm had not only unveiled hidden riches but also revealed the indomitable spirit of a team determined to conquer the challenges that lay beneath the surface.

Mario let out a whoop and pumped his fist in the air as the gold flowed from the sulfide ores. "We did it!" he exclaimed. "I knew we could find gold here."

Pablo nodded in agreement. "Your persistence has paid off, Mario," he said.

"I smiled, feeling a sense of pride and accomplishment wash over me. "It's been a team effort," I said. "We couldn't have done it without everyone's hard work and dedication."

The setting sun painted the sky in hues of orange and pink, casting a warm glow over our campsite. As the crackling flames of the campfire danced to life, we gathered around, a triumphant air enveloping us.

Mario, the architect of our newfound success, stood with a raised glass, the flickering firelight reflecting in his eyes. "To the future," he proclaimed, his voice carrying the weight of our collective dreams. "May this gold bring prosperity and happiness to all those who seek it."

With an air of camaraderie, we clinked our glasses together, the sound resonating through the evening air. The first sip carried the taste of triumph, a flavor as rich and satisfying as the gold we had unearthed. This moment, we knew, would be etched in the annals of our shared history.

As the night deepened, the crackling fire became a beacon of shared accomplishment. The air was filled with laughter and the gentle murmur of conversation. Enrique, a satisfied smile on his face, raised an eyebrow and asked, "So, Mario, any plans for this newfound treasure trove?"

Mario, the eternal optimist, leaned back, the flames dancing in his eyes. "Well, my friends, the possibilities are as vast as the ocean. We could expand the mining operation, invest in the community, or maybe build a monument to our success!"

Pablo, ever the realist, chimed in, "Let's not forget to keep some aside for a rainy day. The future is uncertain, after all."

The night wore on, the stars above witnessing our animated discussions about the potential of our newfound wealth. Dreams were woven into the fabric of our conversations, each word a brushstroke painting a picture of a future shaped by our endeavors.

But for that enchanted evening, as the campfire's glow flickered and cast shadows on our faces, the only certainty was the gold glittering in the firelight—the tangible manifestation of our hard work, determination, and the hope it held for each one of us. It was a night of pure joy, a celebration of success that transcended the boundaries of time and space, forever etched in the tapestry of our shared journey.

18

CHAPTER

The morning after our successful exploration and discovery of gold at Pueblo Viejo, we woke up to the shocking news that Ambassador Martinez had been involved in a terrible car accident. The accident had occurred on his way to meet with El Jefe to discuss our exploration.

We were devastated by the news. Martinez had been a key figure in our expedition, and his support and influence had been instrumental in securing the funding and resources we needed to carry out our mission. We were all worried about his health and safety and wondered what would happen next.

As the day wore on, we learned more details about the accident. It had been a serious collision, and Martinez had suffered some injuries, including a broken leg and a concussion. He was being treated at a nearby hospital, and his condition was stable but critical.

As the days passed, we waited anxiously for news of Martinez's recovery and any updates on our situation. We were unsure of how the accident would affect our plans, and we feared that without Martinez's support, our efforts to extract the gold could be in jeopardy.

We knew we had to carry on with our exploration and with renewed energy and determination, we set out to extract the gold from the sulfide ores using a new method we had developed. It was a challenging and complex process, but we persevered, fueled by the knowledge that our work would bring prosperity and opportunity to our country.

The weight of the devastating news about Ambassador Martinez's demise hung heavy in the air as the sun rose on a somber new day. The camp that had once echoed with the sounds of hope and triumph now bore the hushed tones of mourning. Martinez's passing cast a long shadow over our team, leaving us to grapple not only with the loss of a key ally but also with the harsh reality that our link to El Jefe had been severed.

In the wake of this unexpected tragedy, grief painted our conversations with solemn hues. Mario, his face reflecting both determination and sorrow, spoke up amidst the collective sense of loss. "Martinez wouldn't want us to give up," he asserted. "We owe it to him and ourselves to see this through."

Yet, the harsh truth loomed before us. With Martinez gone, our secret was now buried with him. The corridors of power that had once been open to us were now sealed shut. A palpable tension gripped the team as we faced a crossroads—abandon the mission and surrender our dreams or forge ahead in the shadows, risking everything.

Mario, with fire in his eyes, rallied us. "We can't let Martinez's death be the end of our dreams. We have to keep going—for him and ourselves."

The decision was made to persist in our mission, to continue the operation clandestinely. The risks were glaring, and the consequences of discovery were dire. As we embarked on this covert path, we became shadows in the daylight, working with meticulous precision and unwavering resolve. Every movement, every transaction, was shrouded in secrecy.

Enrique, his eyes reflecting the gravity of the situation, spoke in hushed tones during one of our clandestine meetings. "We're on our own now. We need to be careful, watch each other's backs, and ensure the survival of both our operation and ourselves."

And so, beneath the veil of silence, we toiled in the depths of uncertainty, driven by the memory of Ambassador Martinez and fueled by the hope that our clandestine efforts would one day see the light of acknowledgment. Little did we know that in the shadows, the seeds of both peril and promise were sown, and our journey took an unforeseen turn into the realms of danger and secrecy.

19

CHAPTER

Antonio strolled down El Malecon on a sunny afternoon in Santo Domingo. As he passed by one of the shops, he heard a familiar voice.

"Kike! Is that you?" It was Isabella, the girl he met on the ship during his trip from Italy to the Dominican Republic.

Enrique turned around to see Isabella standing in front of a small sewing shop, holding some fabric. She looked just as beautiful as he remembered.

"Isabella!" he exclaimed, a smile spreading across his face. "It's great to see you again. How have you been?"

"I've been good," she replied, walking over to him. "I'm working as a seamstress now, offering my services to anyone who needs them."

"That's great," Enrique said, impressed by her new venture. "I didn't know you had a talent for sewing."

Isabella smiled. "What about you? How's the Island treating you? Did you find your brother?"

Enrique couldn't help but feel a rush of nostalgia as he looked into Isabella's eyes, the years between them melting away in that moment. "I have a lot of stories to tell you," he replied, a genuine smile playing on his lips. "Can I tell you over coffee?"

That was Enrique's best line to ask for a date. He knew Isabella was the love of his life.

Isabella's eyes sparkled with a mix of curiosity and warmth. "Coffee sounds perfect," she said, a soft chuckle escaping her lips.

As they settled into a cozy café, the aroma of freshly brewed coffee enveloping them, Enrique found himself transported back in time. The clinking of cups and the murmur of other patrons became the backdrop to a story that unfolded between them.

Enrique began, his voice filled with the excitement of a storyteller unveiling long-held secrets. "You wouldn't believe the adventures we had in those mines. The challenges, the triumphs, and, of course, the unexpected twists that kept us on our toes."

Isabella listened with a mix of amusement and genuine interest. "I always knew you were destined for extraordinary things," she teased, a playful glint in her eye.

Enrique chuckled, the lines on his face telling the tales of experiences etched into his memory. "But you, Isabella, you've become quite the entrepreneur. Tell me about your sewing business. It seems you've turned a skill into an art."

Isabella blushed at the compliment, a mixture of pride and humility in her response. "Well, you know, a girl's got to make a living. And sewing has been good to me."

They chatted for hours, catching up on the intricacies of Enrique's mining adventures and discussing the nuances of Isabella's entrepreneurial journey. The café buzzed around them, but in that little corner, time seemed to stand still.

Enrique couldn't help but express his admiration. "Isabella, you've always had this incredible determination. It's one of the things I've always loved about you."

A tender smile played on Isabella's lips. "And you, Enrique, always the adventurer. I've missed hearing your stories."

As they lingered over the last sips of coffee, Enrique felt a warmth spreading through him. Isabella, with her entrepreneurial spirit and unwavering determination, was as captivating as ever. The café had witnessed not just the exchange of stories but the rekindling of a connection that time and distance could not diminish. And in that moment, Enrique knew that the love he felt for Isabella was as timeless as the tales they shared.

"I have to go now," Isabella said, looking at her watch. "I have a client waiting for me. It was great seeing you again, Enrique."

"It was great seeing you too, Isabella," Enrique said, feeling a sense of regret as she walked away. He couldn't help but wonder what could have been if they had met under different circumstances. But he was happy for her and proud of her for following her passion. As he continued down the Malecon, he made a mental note to keep in touch with her and maybe even visit her shop for a custom-made outfit.

20

CHAPTER

Enrique's heart raced as he stood near La Puerta del Conde, the historic gateway that held so many memories. He couldn't believe that fate had brought him back to this place, to the one person who had always held a special space in his heart – Isabella. The air was thick with anticipation as he saw her approaching, and he couldn't help but feel a mixture of excitement and nervousness.

Isabella, with her infectious smile, spotted Enrique waiting near the iconic gate. Her steps quickened, and when she reached him, she greeted him with a warm hug. "Enrique! It's been too long," she exclaimed, her eyes shining with genuine happiness.

Enrique grinned, his eyes reflecting the joy of the moment. "Isabella, you have no idea how much I've missed you."

They strolled together, reminiscing about old times and catching up on the years they had spent apart. La Puerta del Conde, a symbol of Dominican history, stood tall behind them, its stone walls echoing the tales of the past.

As they reached a quiet corner near the gate, Enrique took a deep breath, gathering the courage to express what he had been feeling. "Isabella, there's something I've been wanting to ask you."

Isabella looked at him with curiosity, her brow slightly furrowed. "What is it, Enrique?"

He took her hands in his, his eyes locked onto hers. "Isabella, would you consider living with me? I've realized that life is too short to be apart, and I want to share every moment with you."

A smile spread across Isabella's face, a mixture of surprise and delight. "Enrique, are you asking me to move in with you?"

He nodded a playful glint in his eyes. "Yes, that's exactly what I'm asking. What do you say?"

Isabella laughed, the sound echoing through the quiet space near La Puerta del Conde. "Well, Mr. Adventurer, it's about time you made such a bold move. I'd love to live with you."

Enrique couldn't contain his happiness. "Great! Now, there's just one more thing I've been wanting to do."

Isabella looked at him with curiosity. "And what's that?"

With a mischievous twinkle in his eye, Enrique leaned in, capturing Isabella's lips with his own in a sweet and tender kiss. Laughter bubbled between them, the moment filled with a lightness that only true love could bring.

As they broke the kiss, Enrique grinned. "I've been wanting to do that for a long time."

Isabella playfully nudged him. "Well, it's about time, Mr. Adventurer. Let's see where this new adventure takes us."

And so, near La Puerta del Conde, Enrique and Isabella embarked on a new chapter, their love story continuing with the promise of shared moments and adventures yet to come.

21

CHAPTER

Enrique and Isabella had been living together for a year in a two-floor apartment building very small and modest. The small apartment was nestled in the heart of Santo Domingo, just a stone's throw from the famous El Malecon. Despite its modest size, the apartment was cozy and inviting, with a layout that made the most of its limited space.

As soon as you walked through the door, you were greeted by the warm glow of sunlight streaming in from the floor-to-ceiling windows that framed the stunning view of the sea. The living room was small but comfortable, with a plush sofa and a couple of armchairs arranged around a sleek glass coffee table.

The walls were painted a soft cream color, accented by vibrant pops of color in the form of a few carefully chosen pieces of artwork. A bookshelf on one wall held a collection of books and rocks, and a small desk in the corner provided a quiet space for working or writing.

But the true star of the apartment was the balcony, which ran the length of the living room and offered breathtaking views of the sea. It was the perfect spot for sipping coffee in the morning or enjoying a glass of wine in the evening, with the sound of the waves providing a soothing soundtrack to the day.

Despite its small size, the apartment had everything you needed for a comfortable and enjoyable stay in Santo Domingo. And with its prime location just steps from El Malecon, it was the perfect spot for soaking up all that this vibrant city had to offer.

One sunny morning, as Enrique sipped his coffee and perused the morning newspaper, his eyes fell upon the pages of a Batman comic strip. The image of the caped crusader, with his sleek costume and iconic utility belt, sparked an idea in Enrique's adventurous mind.

As he studied the cartoon outfit, an unconventional thought crossed his mind – a belt, not for crime-fighting gadgets, but for smuggling gold. The concept of a discreet, specially designed belt to transport precious cargo intrigued him. He envisioned a way to covertly carry powdered gold through airport security, inspired by the secrecy of the Dark Knight's utility belt.

Unable to contain his excitement, Enrique rushed to find Isabella, who was busy with her sewing work. Bursting into the bedroom with the newspaper in hand, he exclaimed, "Isabella, you won't believe what I found!"

Isabella looked up from her sewing machine, a curious expression on her face. "What is it, Enrique? You seem unusually excited."

Enrique spread out the newspaper, pointing at the Batman comic strip. "Look at this! Batman's utility belt. I've got an idea – a belt to smuggle gold. A discreet way to get it to Italy!"

Isabella's eyes widened with surprise and amusement. "Enrique, you're like a real-life superhero with your creative schemes. Tell me more about this belt idea."

Enrique eagerly explained his plan, detailing how the belt could be designed to conceal powdered gold and pass-through airport security undetected. Isabella, always supportive of Enrique's adventurous endeavors, couldn't help but be intrigued by the audacious concept.

Isabella was hesitant at first. "I don't know, Enrique. That sounds risky."

"I know, but it's the only way we can get the gold to Italy," he said. "And with your skills, I know we can do it."

After a moment of contemplation, Isabella grinned. "Well, it's certainly a unique idea. Let's get to work on this special belt of yours. But promise me, no capes – we're not going for the full superhero look!"

Enrique laughed, appreciating Isabella's good humor. "No capes, I promise. Just a belt that will make our gold-smuggling operation a bit more... stylish."

And so, armed with the inspiration from a comic strip and fueled by their shared creativity, Enrique and Isabella set to work on crafting a belt that would play a crucial role in their unconventional quest for prosperity and adventure. Little did they know that their ingenious creation would become an essential part of their daring exploits.

Finally, they had a working prototype.

"I think it's going to work," Enrique said, admiring the belt.

"Thank you, Bella. I couldn't have done this without you."

Isabella smiled, feeling a sense of satisfaction from her handiwork. "Just promise me you'll be careful," she said.

"I will," he replied, kissing her on the forehead. "I promise."

They hugged each other tightly, knowing the risks they were taking. But for them, it was worth it to have a chance at a better life.

Using her skills, Isabella designed a belt that had multiple hidden compartments where the powder gold could be stored.

Enrique was amazed at her work and tested the belt himself, feeling the weight of the gold within.

22

CHAPTER

The day had arrived for Enrique to put his ingenious plan into action. Nervously, he strapped on the specially crafted belt that held a discreet compartment for the powdered gold. The airport loomed ahead, a bustling hub of activity.

Enrique's heart raced as he approached the security checkpoint. Isabella had done an excellent job in designing the belt – it looked ordinary, inconspicuous, just like any other belt a traveler might wear. However, the weight of the powdered gold pressed against his waist, a constant reminder of the danger he carried. Each step felt heavier, each breath shallower, as he neared the uniformed officer.

As he stood in line, he couldn't shake the feeling of being watched. Each step closer to the security guard intensified his anxiety. Thoughts of potential complications filled his mind, but he pushed them aside, reminding himself that this was the only way to secure their newfound wealth.

When Enrique reached to show his passport, he took a deep breath and stepped forward. The belt, hidden beneath his shirt, went through without raising suspicion. Relief washed over him, but the ordeal wasn't over.

Just as he thought he had passed through unnoticed, an airport security officer approached him. "Señor, me acompaña por favor". He wanted to follow him to perform a secondary inspection.

Enrique's heart sank. Despite his attempts to remain calm, a bead of sweat formed on his forehead. He followed the officer to a separate area, where he was subjected to a thorough inspection.

The security officer scrutinized every inch of Enrique's belongings, his hands hovering over the belt. Enrique's mind raced, contemplating the consequences of being caught. But the officer, seemingly satisfied, allowed him to proceed.

As Enrique walked toward the departure gate, he couldn't believe his luck. The close call had rattled him, but he had successfully navigated the hurdles of airport security. His plan, daring as it was, had worked.

Once on the plane, he felt a mix of relief and exhilaration. The powdered gold was safely stowed, and he was on his way to Italy. Enrique couldn't help but marvel at the audacity of their operation. The belt, a symbol of their unconventional journey, had proven to be a crucial element in transporting their wealth discreetly.

Enrique would repeat this nerve-wracking process on subsequent flights, each time relying on the cleverly designed belt and the meticulous work of

Isabella. As he landed in Italy, he knew that their secret operation continued to unfold, hidden beneath the surface of ordinary travel.

Their plan was successful, and they were able to make a considerable profit from their smuggling operation. Enrique and Isabella were thrilled with their success and continued to smuggle gold to Italy keeping it a secret from everyone.

As they sat in their small house, counting their profits, Enrique looked at Isabella with admiration. "Bella, you are amazing," he said. "I couldn't have done this without you."

Isabella smiled back at him, feeling a sense of pride in her work. "We make a great team," she said.

Enrique wrapped his arms around her, holding her close. "I love you," he said.

Isabella leaned into his embrace, feeling grateful for the life they had built together. "I love you too, I'm pregnant," she said.

Enrique's eyes widened in surprise. "Pregnant?" he repeated. "Are you sure?"

Isabella nodded. "I just found out yesterday," she said, tears starting to form in her eyes.

Enrique took her hand in his. "Bella, this is wonderful news," he said, smiling at her. "We're going to have a baby."

Isabella looked up at him, her heart filling with love and hope. "I know," she said, a small smile spreading across her face.

Enrique hugged her tightly, feeling a rush of joy and excitement. "Bella, I'm so happy," he said. "We'll make it work."

Enrique sat on the couch in their small living room, his mind racing with thoughts of their future. Isabella stood nervously by the window; her hands clasped together in front of her.

"I can't believe we're going to be parents," Enrique said, breaking the silence between them.

Isabella turned to face him, a small smile on her face. "I know," she said softly. "It's a lot to take in."

Enrique stood up and walked over to her, wrapping his arms around her waist. "But we'll figure it out," he said. "We always do."

Isabella leaned her head against his chest, feeling the warmth of his embrace. "I just don't want to be a burden," she said, her voice barely above a whisper.

Enrique pulled back slightly, looking into her eyes. "You're not a burden, Bella," he said firmly. "You and our baby are the most important things in the world to me."

Isabella's eyes filled with tears, and she buried her face in his chest once again. "I'm scared," she admitted.

Enrique held her tightly, his heart breaking at the sound of her fear. "I know," he said softly. "But we'll face it together. And we'll be okay."

They stood there for a few moments, holding each other and basking in the warmth of their love. Finally, Isabella pulled back and looked up at him, a hint of determination in her eyes.

"You know what?" she said. "I have an idea. Let's name our baby after your brother. That's the reason you are here and why we met on a ship."

Enrique smiled at her, feeling a sense of pride and awe. "I think that's a beautiful idea," he said.

"Mario," Isabella said, her voice filled with conviction. "Mario Costa."

Enrique nodded, feeling a sense of reverence for the name. "Mario Costa," he repeated. "I like it."

Isabella smiled, feeling a sense of hope for their future. No matter what challenges lay ahead, she knew that with Enrique by her side, they could face them together.

Isabella nodded, feeling grateful to have him by her side. She knew that the road ahead would be difficult, but with Enrique and their baby, she felt like she could overcome any obstacle.

23

CHAPTER

Enrique had always wanted to do something special for Isabella. With the excitement of the baby on the way and the stress of the upcoming smuggling job to Italy, he decided that it was the perfect time to give her a surprise.

Isabella couldn't believe her eyes when Enrique pulled up in front of their small house with a brand new 1960 Chevrolet Bel Air. The car was a beauty, with its sleek, silver body and gleaming chrome accents that sparkled in the sunlight. As she walked around the car, she ran her hand over the smooth finish, admiring the attention to detail that went into its design.

The car's interior was just as impressive, with plush seats covered in soft, white leather that made her feel like she was sitting on a cloud. Isabella couldn't help but smile as she looked at the dashboard, with its shiny knobs and dials that glowed like jewels in the dark.

But what made the car stand out to Isabella was its powerful engine. As Enrique revved it up, she could feel the energy and excitement pulsing through her veins. It was like the car had a life of its own, and she couldn't wait to hit the open road with it.

"Kike, this is amazing," she said, tears of joy welling up in her eyes. "I can't believe it."

Enrique grinned at her reaction. "I wanted to give you something special," he said. "Something to remember while I'm away."

Isabella hugged him tightly, feeling grateful for his generosity. They spent the rest of the day driving around in the new car, exploring the city, and enjoying their time together.

However, just two weeks after Enrique left for Italy, Isabella's frustration reached a boiling point as she stared at the stalled car on the side of the road. She had tried every trick in the book to revive the stubborn engine, but it remained resolutely silent. Exasperated, she slammed the car door shut and decided to abandon it, choosing to walk back home instead.

With determination in her stride, Isabella began the journey on foot. The sun beat down on her as she made her way along the familiar route, the disappointment of the stalled car lingering in her thoughts. As she walked, a passing neighbor slowed down and rolled down the window.

"Isabella, everything okay?" inquired Mrs. Rodriguez, concern etched on her face.

Isabella nodded, forcing a smile. "Car trouble. I've left it there for now. Maybe I'll get a tow later."

Mrs. Rodriguez offered her a ride, but Isabella politely declined, choosing to embrace the walk as a chance to clear her mind. The rhythmic tap of her heels on the pavement became a contemplative soundtrack, and with each step, she felt a bit of the frustration dissipate.

Upon reaching home, Isabella's mind was already shifting gears. Instead of dwelling on the mechanical hiccup, she saw an opportunity to embrace the simple act of walking, a chance to slow down and appreciate the surroundings. The incident became a reminder that sometimes, unexpected detours could lead to unexpected discoveries.

Isabella opted to sell the car, affixing a "For Sale" sign on the windshield with the hope of making the best of the situation. To her surprise, she received a call that very afternoon. The attractive price for a nearly brand-new car had caught someone's eye, and soon enough, she successfully sold the vehicle.

A few days later, she received a call from the new owner of the car. "Ms. Isabella, I'm sorry to bother you, but I think you should know that your car is perfectly fine," the man said.

"What do you mean?" Isabella asked, confused.

"Well, it seems like it just ran out of gas," the man explained. "I filled it up and it started right up without a problem."

Isabella couldn't believe what she was hearing. All this time, she had been worrying and stressing over a simple mistake. She laughed at herself and felt a bit foolish but was relieved to know that the car was okay.

She decided to use the money from the sale to buy something practical for the baby but still thought fondly of the Chevrolet and the special memories it had given her and Enrique.

24

CHAPTER

Isabella sat at her sewing machine, the soft hum of the motor filling the small apartment. She ran her hands over the fabric, feeling the smooth texture of the silk. She had always loved to sew, ever since she was a young girl in her mother's dress shop. And now, with her own business, she was living her dream.

Enrique walked into the room, a smile on his face. "How's business?"

"Great," Isabella replied, beaming. "I just got an order from the Café Santo Domingo. They want custom uniforms for all their employees."

Enrique chuckled. "Looks like you're becoming quite the businesswoman."

Isabella grinned. "I'm just getting started."

As they looked out the window, they could see the sea sparkling in the distance. The apartment was small and modest, but it had a great view of the sea, just a few meters from El Malecon.

All of a sudden Enrique whispered in Isabella's ears "I have a surprise, Let's go".

Enrique led Isabella and Mario to their new home, a charming abode nestled on Avenida Villaespesa. The house, with its vibrant facade adorned with blooming bougainvillea, stood as a testament to their dreams materializing. As they approached, the scent of freshly brewed coffee from Café Santo Domingo, the renowned coffee roaster nearby, wafted through the air, creating an atmosphere of bustling urban life.

Upon entering, the house revealed a cozy interior, filled with warm hues and tasteful furnishings. Isabella's eyes lit up as she took in the inviting living space, and she couldn't help but admire the details Enrique had put into making it a comfortable home for their family.

In the kitchen, the aroma of Isabella's favorite Dominican dishes filled the air, a delightful reminder of the warmth and love that now surrounded them. The house seemed to echo with the laughter of Mario, adding a joyful soundtrack to their newfound life.

As they explored each room, Isabella discovered that Enrique had thoughtfully set up a small sewing studio for her, anticipating her entrepreneurial spirit. The walls adorned with vibrant fabrics and the hum of sewing machines echoed the creativity and determination that fueled Isabella's aspirations.

Seated in the living room, Enrique smiled at Isabella. "I wanted our home to be a place where we can build our dreams together," he said, his eyes reflecting pride and love.

Isabella, still absorbing the reality of their achievements, responded with gratitude, "Enrique, it's more than I could have imagined. I can't wait to see what the future holds for us."

Their journey was just beginning, and with La Fantasia, the boutique Isabella had opened next door, she was ready to make her mark in the burgeoning industries of the city. The air buzzed with the promise of success and the sweet scent of coffee, encapsulating the essence of their shared dreams and accomplishments.

One night Enrique sat down beside her, taking her hand. "I'm proud of you, you know that?"

Isabella leaned in and kissed him. "And I'm proud of you too. You've been working so hard to support us."

Enrique smiled. "It's worth it to see you happy."

As they sat together, they knew that their new life was just beginning. And with Isabella's business taking off, they were excited to see where it would take them.

25

CHAPTER

After three long years of exploring the depths of the gold mine, the team stumbled upon a rare and unexpected discovery—uranium. Pablo was the first to recognize the faint greenish glow of the ore, his face paling as he realized what it meant. Enrique and Mario crowded around, their excitement quickly turning to dread. They knew the implications: uranium was a treasure far more dangerous than gold, and it would draw the attention of powers far beyond their control.

They knew that uranium was a highly regulated and dangerous material, and the consequences of being caught with it could be severe.

Pablo spoke up first, his voice filled with concern. "Guys, we have a big problem. This uranium could get us all in serious trouble."

Enrique nodded in agreement, his mind racing with the potential risks. "We need to be careful with how we handle this. We can't let anyone know about it."

Mario chimed in; his brow furrowed in thought. "But how are we going to hide it? The government is going to find out eventually."

Pablo rubbed his chin, thinking hard. "We need to come up with a plan. Maybe we can sell it to someone in secret or hide it somewhere no one will ever find it."

Enrique shook his head. "We can't sell it. That's even riskier. And hiding it is too dangerous. What if someone accidentally stumbles upon it?"

Mario sighed heavily. "I don't know what we're going to do. This is a nightmare."

The three men sat in silence for a few moments, contemplating their next move. They knew that they had stumbled upon something big, but the risks were too high to handle on their own. They needed to act fast and come up with a plan before their discovery was discovered by the wrong people.

Word of their discovery quickly spread in town, and it wasn't long before the news reached the ears of El Jefe himself. The team knew that they were in trouble. El Jefe was not known for his leniency towards those who crossed him or threatened his power.

The team was called to a meeting with El Jefe at "El Palacio Nacional", and they knew it was a matter of life or death. They were prepared to do whatever it took to protect themselves and their families.

As they entered the meeting room, they saw El Jefe sitting at the head of the table, a stern expression on his face. He greeted them with a nod but didn't waste any time getting to the point.

"I hear that you have found something very interesting in the mine," he said, his voice cold and calculated.

The team exchanged uneasy glances, unsure of how to proceed.

"Yes, we found some uranium," Mario finally spoke up, his voice shaking slightly.

El Jefe's expression remained unchanged, but his eyes grew colder. "And what do you plan to do with this information?" he asked.

The team knew that they had to tread carefully. They couldn't risk angering El Jefe, but they also couldn't stay silent and let him exploit the uranium for his own gain.

"We were planning to report the findings to the appropriate authorities," one of the team members said, trying to sound confident.

El Jefe leaned back in his chair; his eyes still fixed on the team. "I see," he said, his voice dripping with skepticism. "And what makes you think that I will allow you to do that?"

The team felt their hearts sink. They knew that they were in a difficult situation. But they also knew that they couldn't back down now.

"We have to report this," another team member said, his voice firmer than before. "It's a matter of public safety."

El Jefe narrowed his eyes, but the team stood their ground. They knew that they were taking a huge risk, but they also knew that they couldn't stay silent.

Finally, after what felt like hours of tense silence, El Jefe spoke. "Very well," he said, his voice low and menacing. "Make sure this finding of yours doesn't damage my governance. I only see Nickle in what you have shown me. Remember this: if anything happens to me or my operation, you will be the first to pay the price."

The team knew that they were in for a dangerous ride, but they also knew that they had made the right decision. They left the meeting with a sense of relief and apprehension, unsure of what the future held. But one thing was for sure: they had found something that could change the course of their lives forever.

After the initial shock wore off, the team knew they had to tread carefully. They were aware of the dangers associated with uranium mining, and the last thing they wanted was to attract unwanted attention from the government or other groups.

"We can't just leave the uranium there," Pablo said, his voice filled with concern. "We have to report it."

"We can't do that," Enrique replied, shaking his head. "We all know what will happen if we do. We'll be shut down, or worse, targeted by the wrong people."

Mario spoke up, "We need to find a way to keep this a secret. The agreement with El Jefe was to tell everyone we found Nickel instead."

"But what about the risks associated with uranium?" Pablo asked.

"We'll take extra precautions," Enrique said firmly. "We'll make sure everyone wears protective gear, and we'll limit our exposure to the mineral. We'll be careful."

The team agreed, and they spent the next few days devising a plan to mine the uranium safely and keep it a secret. They knew the stakes were high, and they couldn't afford to make any mistakes. It was a risky move, but they were determined to make it work.

26

CHAPTER

Tony's eyes got wider as he kept reading his grandfather's diary.

Tony had been pouring over his grandfather's diaries for hours, unable to tear himself away from the pages. His grandfather had been a man of many talents, and his life story was nothing short of fascinating. Tony was amazed at how much he had learned about his family's history and his roots.

As he read, he couldn't help but wonder if there was any clue in the diaries that could help him uncover the truth about his father's death. He had always suspected that there was more to the story than what his mother had told him, and the diaries seemed like the perfect place to start.

Tony kept reading, page after page, lost in his thoughts.

As he continued to read, Tony felt a sudden pang of regret that he had never had the chance to know his grandfather better. He had passed away before Tony was born, and he realized now just how much he had missed out on.

But as he turned the pages, Tony's focus shifted back to his mission. He was determined to find out the truth about his father's death, and he was convinced that the answers were hidden somewhere in these pages.

"Could it be that my father's death was somehow related to the Uranium findings?" Tony muttered to himself as he read.

He scanned the pages intently, searching for any clue that might lead him closer to the truth. The more he read, the more he realized just how complex his family's history was.

As the hours ticked by, Tony continued to read, completely absorbed in his grandfather's life story. He knew that he still had a long way to go before he found the answers he was looking for, but for the first time in a long time, he felt a sense of hope that he might just be able to uncover the truth after all.

27

CHAPTER

One afternoon, as Pablo was taking a smoke break outside the mine entrance, he noticed a man he didn't recognize approaching him. The man introduced himself as Jose Rodriguez, a reporter for the Listin Diario, and asked if he could ask him a few questions about the mine and the work being done there.

"Solo unas preguntas por favor" said the reporter with a smirk on his face.

Pablo was hesitant at first, but eventually agreed to answer his questions. Jose asked about the types of minerals they were extracting, how much they were producing, and who was in charge of overseeing the operation. Pablo tried to keep his answers vague and non-committal, but he could sense that Jose was digging for more information.

After a few more minutes of questioning, Jose suddenly brought up the topic of uranium. Pablo was taken aback and tried to brush it off, saying that they had only found small traces of it in the mine. But Jose persisted, asking if there was any chance that they had found enough uranium to be valuable.

Pablo's heart raced as he realized that the reporter was onto their secret. He knew that he had to be careful with his words, but he couldn't lie to him. Finally, he admitted that they had found a significant amount of uranium in the mine.

Jose's eyes widened in excitement, and he started scribbling notes furiously in his notepad. "This is big news," he said. "The people have a right to know about this discovery."

Pablo's stomach turned as he realized the consequences of this revelation. If the government found out about their discovery, they could be in grave danger. He knew that he had to warn the rest of the team and figure out a way to protect their find.

The team's paranoia grew as they felt like they were being watched constantly. They had no way of knowing if anyone had discovered their secret discovery of uranium. They tried to maintain a low profile and kept their work as discreet as possible.

The team tried to evade any questioning about the mine and any findings. The situation became more worrisome when the reporter published his findings in the newspaper, highlighting the government's apparent cover-up of the mine's hazardous materials.

Soon enough, the town began to feel the effects of the uranium discovery. The river water near the mine was contaminated with uranium and was causing people to fall ill. The situation escalated quickly, and the team realized they needed to act fast to protect their discovery and their lives.

But the risks were high, and they were up against a dangerous dictator who would stop at nothing to maintain his power. The team had to navigate the treacherous political landscape to keep their discovery hidden and protect themselves from the wrath of the government.

They knew that they had to come up with a plan to protect their discovery and the people of the town. Mario contacted a friend in the United States who specialized in environmental law and began to work with him to develop a strategy to protect their interests.

The team was on high alert and always looking over their shoulders, knowing that their secret was at risk of being exposed at any moment. The tension was palpable, and the stakes were high as they worked to protect their discovery and their lives.

28

CHAPTER

Enrique knew that the discovery of Uranium would cause trouble, but he never imagined the extent of it. When he received the call from Pablo about the reporter's investigation and the sickness of the townspeople, he knew that their secret was out.

Enrique immediately alerted Isabella and instructed her to go with their son Mario to Rome with his sister. He knew that it was no longer safe for them to stay on the island. They had to get out, and they had to do it fast.

"Isabella, listen to me carefully," he said over the phone. "I need you to pack your bags and go with Mario to Rome. I'll meet you there as soon as I can."

"Enrique, what's going on?" Isabella asked, her voice filled with fear.

"They are coming after us," Enrique said, his voice trembling. "You have to leave the country before they come after you and Mario."

Isabella didn't hesitate. She knew that she had to do what Enrique said. She packed their bags and left with Mario and Enrique's sister that same day.

However, El Jefe found out about the Americans' involvement. The dictator was furious and threatened to throw the team in jail for espionage.

Enrique knew that they were in serious trouble. He couldn't risk Isabella and Mario getting caught, so he sent Isabella and his son Mario to Rome. But he had to stay behind and face the consequences of their actions.

In the middle of the night, secret police showed up at Enrique's house. Enrique's heart raced as he watched the secret police approach him. He knew that he was in trouble, but he had no idea how much trouble he was in.

"Enrique Costa," one of the officers said, his voice cold and stern. "Venga con nosotros, Estas arrestado" and took him to Cárcel La Victoria. The Victoria Prison was the brand-new prison created by El Jefe where political prisoners were held and, it was used on several occasions as a punishment center, to which political prisoners from prisons in other regions of the country were brought. This jail was a disciplinary facility.

He was interrogated for hours about their discovery, and he refused to reveal anything. He knew that their lives were at stake, and he couldn't risk his family's safety.

Enrique was brought to a dimly lit room where he was interrogated by two stern-looking men. One of them introduced himself as Colonel Diaz, head of the Dominican Secret Police.

"Mr. Costa, we have reason to believe that you are involved in espionage activities," Colonel Diaz began, his voice firm and unwavering.

Enrique raised an eyebrow in surprise. "Espionage? I don't understand, Colonel. I'm just a Geologist."

The other man, who had remained silent until now, leaned forward and spoke in a menacing tone. "Don't play dumb with us, Costa. We know that you have been working with the Americans. And we want to know everything."

Enrique shook his head in disbelief. "I don't know what you're talking about. I have no connection to any intelligence agencies."

Colonel Diaz slammed his hand on the table. "Stop lying to us, Costa! We know that you have been smuggling uranium out of the country. And we believe that you are the one working with the Americans to undermine our government."

Enrique felt a wave of panic wash over him. He had heard rumors of the government cracking down on anyone suspected of collaborating with foreign powers. He knew that if he was labeled as a spy, he would face serious consequences.

"I swear to you, Colonel, I am not a spy. I am just a Geologist trying to make a living," Enrique pleaded.

The two men exchanged a look before Colonel Diaz spoke again. "We will be keeping a close eye on you, Mr. Costa. And if we find any evidence of your involvement in espionage, you will be dealt with accordingly."

Enrique felt a sense of relief wash over him as he was escorted out of the room. He knew that he had to be careful from now on, as he was now under close surveillance by the government.

Days turned into weeks, and Enrique was still being held captive. He had no idea what was happening to Isabella and Mario, and he feared the worst. He tried to stay strong, but the constant interrogation and confinement were taking a toll on him.

Meanwhile, Isabella and Mario were safe at their home being watched by "calieses" who were Trujillo's regime spies in the neighborhood. Even though safe, Isabella couldn't help but worry about Enrique. She knew that he was in danger, and she prayed that he would make it out alive.

29

CHAPTER

Enrique's time in La Victoria prison had been a challenging and trying experience. The days stretched endlessly, marked by harsh conditions, violence, and uncertainty. However, amid the darkness of the prison, he had heard stories that shed light on the horrors faced by others. Among the tales that circulated the prison cells, one particular story had left an indelible mark on his memory.

The story begins with a group of Greek foreigners who had been lured to the Dominican Republic with the promise of jobs and a better life. These men had arrived in the country with hope in their hearts, eager to provide for their families back home.

As the weeks passed, their initial optimism had given way to despair. They had been promised employment but were quickly coerced into an unexpected and brutal role: members of Trujillo's foreign legion. Instead of finding jobs and stability, they were forced into service as soldiers, fighting for a regime they neither understood nor supported.

When they refused to comply with their orders, the consequences had been severe. The foreigners had been subjected to unimaginable cruelty. They were stripped of their clothing and thrown into communal and solitary cells within the unforgiving walls of La Victoria prison, located outside Ciudad Trujillo.

Inside those cold, dim cells, the Greeks had endured suffering beyond words. They were given meager rations of slop and left to fend for themselves in the squalid conditions. The prison guards showed no mercy, routinely beating the men unconscious with clubs and wire whips.

One of the most heinous forms of torture involved scalding the Greeks with boiling water, leaving them with painful and disfiguring burns. The purpose was clear: to break their spirits, force their compliance, and turn them into instruments of the regime.

While treatment improved slightly for those who agreed to serve in Trujillo's foreign legion, the Greeks had held firm to their principles. For two long months, they had resisted the pressures to enlist, remaining resolute in their refusal to partake in the violent and oppressive regime.

It was only when the Greek embassy in Washington intervened and negotiated on their behalf that their ordeal came to an end. The foreigners were finally granted their freedom, and released from the clutches of La Victoria prison.

Enrique, as he listened to this harrowing tale, felt a deep sense of empathy for those who had endured such unimaginable suffering. Their story served as a stark reminder of the horrors inflicted by the oppressive regime, and it fueled his determination to ensure the safety and well-being of his own family.

As he spent his days in La Victoria prison, Enrique couldn't help but wonder about the fate of the Greek strangers. Had they been able to return to their homeland, reunite with their families, and find solace and justice for the atrocities they had endured? The answers were unknown, but their story remained etched in his memory as a testament to the resilience of the human spirit in the face of unspeakable adversity.

30

CHAPTER

Enrique had spent six long months in La Victoria Jail, and it had taken its toll on him. But finally, he was being released, and he couldn't wait to be reunited with his family. After six months and one day, he was released, but he knew that he couldn't stay in the country any longer. He had to leave before the secret police came after him again.

As he walked out of the prison gates, he saw his brother Mario waiting for him.

"Mario, it's good to see you," Enrique said, embracing his younger brother.

"You too, hermano," Mario replied. "Pablo is waiting for us with a boat."

With the help of his cousin Pablo, Mario planned to escape the country on a small boat departing from the shores of Miches. It was a risky move, but they had no other choice.

Enrique nodded, grateful for his brother's help. "Let's go, then," he said, following Mario towards the gates.

As they walked out of the prison compound, Enrique felt a sense of relief wash over him. He was finally free, and he could start his life anew.

"So, how did you manage to get the boat?" Enrique asked Mario as they made their way towards the shore.

"We had to pay a pretty penny for it, but it was worth it," Mario replied. "Pablo arranged everything.

He's been working hard to make sure we can get out of here."

Enrique nodded, grateful for Pablo's help as well. "I owe him my life," he said.

As they reached the shore, Enrique saw a small boat waiting for them. He could see Pablo standing next to it, looking out towards the horizon.

"Pablo!" Enrique called out, waving his arms.

Pablo turned around and smiled when he saw Enrique and Mario. "Cousin, you made it," he said, walking over to them.

"Thanks to you," Enrique replied, hugging him.

Pablo shook his head. "Don't mention it. We're family, and family takes care of each other."

Enrique nodded, feeling grateful for his cousin's help. "Let's go, then," he said, climbing into the boat.

The night was dark, and the only light came from the stars above and the distant glow of the city lights on the shoreline. As the small boat set off into the dark waters, Enrique couldn't help but feel a mix of emotions. He was leaving behind everything he had ever known, but he also knew that he was doing it to protect the people he loved.

As they sailed through the night, their hopes high and their destination uncertain, the sound of the waves crashing against the boat's hull provided a comforting rhythm. They sailed deeper into international waters, leaving the Dominican Republic behind.

However, their hopes of a smooth escape were soon shattered. Just as they began to believe they had evaded any pursuers, a sharp spotlight cut through the darkness, blinding them. The roar of an approaching vessel filled the night air.

Enrique's heart sank as he realized what was happening. The American coastguard had spotted them in American waters, and they were now in pursuit.

Panic washed over them as they tried to figure out their next move. Mario grabbed a walkie-talkie and frantically attempted to reach out to Pablo, who was at the helm.

"Pablo, we have company! The coastguard is chasing us!" Mario's voice trembled with fear.

Pablo's hands tightened on the boat's wheel, his eyes scanning the dark horizon. "Hold on tight, everyone! We'll do our best to outrun them!"

The boat surged forward, the engine roaring as Pablo skillfully navigated the waves. But the coastguard vessel was closing in, its powerful searchlight bearing down on them.

Enrique clung to the side of the boat, his heart pounding. "We can't get caught now," he muttered to himself. "Not after coming so far."

As the tension on the boat escalated, the coastguard hailed them over a loudspeaker, ordering them to stop and prepare to be boarded.

Pablo's knuckles turned white as he tightened his grip on the wheel. "We have to make a decision, and we have to make it fast," he said, his voice steady despite the urgency of the situation.

The escape had taken a perilous turn, and the outcome was far from certain. With the coastguard closing in, Enrique, Mario, and Pablo had to rely on their wits and determination to evade capture and reach the safety of international waters.

The deafening roar of the coastguard vessel's engine filled the night air as it closed in on the small boat. Its powerful searchlight pierced the darkness, casting an eerie glow over the water. Panic spread like wildfire among those on board as the reality of their situation sank in.

Enrique's heart pounded in his chest as he clutched the side of the boat, his fingers white-knuckled. He glanced at Mario, who was desperately trying to stay calm.

Pablo, at the helm, knew that their chances of escaping were growing slimmer by the second. He navigated the boat skillfully, but it was clear that the coastguard vessel was closing in fast.

As the two boats neared each other, the searchlight's blinding glare intensified. Enrique squinted against the harsh light, his heart pounding louder in his ears with each passing moment. He could hear the water lapping against the hull, the distant cries of seagulls overhead, and the urgent radio chatter of the approaching coastguard.

"Prepare to be boarded!" a voice boomed over a loudspeaker from the coastguard vessel. "Cut your engine and raise your hands!"

Panic gripped them all. Enrique knew that they had no choice but to comply. He looked at Pablo, his expression resigned. "We have to do as they say," he said.

Pablo nodded, his jaw set with determination. He eased off the throttle, and the boat's engine sputtered to silence. The small vessel bobbed on the dark waves, helpless in the face of the approaching coastguard.

Coastguard officers, armed and clad in dark uniforms, descended onto the small boat, their flashlights cutting through the night. Their faces were stern, their orders curt and unyielding.

"Everyone, hands up!" one of the officers barked as they moved swiftly through the boat. Their flashlights swept over the huddled family, momentarily blinding them.

Enrique, Mario, and Pablo raised their hands, their faces etched with a mixture of fear and resignation.

The officers wasted no time. They quickly assessed the situation, securing everyone on board and confiscating any communication devices they found.

Enrique's heart sank as he watched their chances of escape slip away.

With their hands bound, they were taken into custody by the coastguard officers, their boat now tethered to the larger vessel. Everyone exchanged worried glances, their uncertainty hanging heavy in the air.

As they were led away, Enrique couldn't help but wonder about their fate. What would happen to them now that they were in the custody? The future was uncertain, and the consequences of their actions were yet to be revealed.

31

CHAPTER

Enrique had experienced dread, uncertainty, and loneliness throughout his confinement at La Victoria jail. The walls of his cell were damp, the air thick with the stench of sweat and despair. He would often sit on the cold floor, tracing the cracks in the stone with his fingers, as he revisited the decisions that had brought him here. Each memory—Isabella's smile, Mario's laughter, the glint of gold in the mine—felt like a knife twisting in his chest.

His mind was troubled by one especially distinct recollection, that of the day Trujillo had paid them a visit in a dimly lighted room underneath the prison. The dictator's presence had left a long shadow over their lives, making the event seem strange. It had been a clandestine meeting, and Enrique, Mario, and Pablo had been ushered into a small, windowless chamber. The air was heavy with tension, and the walls seemed to close in around them as they awaited the arrival of the ruthless dictator.

Trujillo's presence was oppressive as soon as he entered the space. He was a guy of great authority and power, and the three men were staring into his icy, analytical eyes. There was an unwritten agreement that he was responsible for their destiny.

The dictator, his voice low and commanding, addressed Mario directly. "Tienes algo que yo quiero," Trujillo said, his voice low and menacing. "You have something I want." His eyes, cold and calculating, bore into Mario, leaving no room for defiance.

Mario, though fearful, met Trujillo's gaze. "What is it that you want, Generalissimo?" he asked cautiously.

Trujillo's lips curled into a chilling smile. "The gold," he replied. "All of it. I want you to ensure that every ounce of that precious metal is extracted from the Pueblo Viejo mine."

Mario paused, his thoughts whirling He understood that complying with Trujillo's requests would entail joining the tyrant in exploiting the mine. However, he was also aware that it may be their only opportunity to preserve his family's safety and independence.

"What do we get in return?" Mario questioned, his voice wavering.

Trujillo leaned in closer, his eyes locking onto Mario's. "Your life," he whispered. "You, your brother, and your cousin will be released from this wretched place. You'll be free to go wherever you please."

The room seemed to close in around them as Mario contemplated the offer. Their freedom hung in the balance, a tantalizing but tainted prize.

Mario glanced at Enrique and Pablo, his mind made up. He knew that agreeing to the deal would come at a great cost, but he couldn't bear to see his family suffer any longer.

"We agree," Mario finally said, his voice steady. "We'll ensure that the gold is extracted from the mine."

Trujillo's smile widened, revealing the depths of his satisfaction. The dark deal had been struck, and the fate of the three men was sealed. In exchange for their freedom, they had become willing participants in the dictator's exploitation of the gold mine.

As they left the dimly lit room, Enrique couldn't help but feel a mixture of relief and remorse. The path to their freedom was clear, but it was tainted by their involvement in Trujillo's schemes.

In the days that followed, Mario, Enrique, and Pablo worked tirelessly to meet their end of the bargain. They oversaw the extraction of gold from the Pueblo Viejo mine, watching as the precious metal was transported away to serve the dictator's insatiable appetite for wealth and power.

However, their agreement with Trujillo came with a caveat. They would be free, but they would have to agree to be deported to Italy once their task was complete. The dictator had ensured that they would never reveal the secrets of the mine or the extent of his exploitation.

As they toiled under the oppressive regime, the promise of freedom was a distant beacon, a glimmer of hope in the darkness. Yet, it came at a heavy price, and the burden of their choices weighed heavily on their hearts.

32

CHAPTER

Enrique's voice quivered with exhaustion and frustration as he addressed his fellow laborers deep within the mountain's belly. The oppressive heat and the ceaseless grind of labor weighed heavily on him, but the promise of freedom fueled his resolve.

"We've come this far," he declared, his voice echoing through the dimly lit tunnel. "We've faced hardships that would break most, but we're still here, together. Remember why we're doing this, why we endure these conditions—it's for our families and our future."

The workers around him nodded in silent agreement, their faces etched with determination. They knew that the colossal tunnel they were constructing was not just a physical monument; it was a symbol of their defiance and hope.

As the days turned into weeks and weeks into months, Enrique, leading his team, marveled at the sheer scale of the tunnel. It seemed as though it would extend to the very heart of the earth. The air was thick with dust and the smell of sweat, but their spirits remained unbroken.

With each pick of the pickaxe, the scrape of shovels against rock, and the thud of hammers on stone, they pressed forward. The dictator's presence loomed like a specter over them, and they understood the price of non-compliance all too well.

Enrique's thoughts often turned to his family, to Isabella and their son Mario. They were the reason he had made the agonizing decision to accept Trujillo's deal. The promise of safety and freedom for his loved ones was the ember of hope that kept him going.

As the tunnel neared completion, he couldn't help but feel a mix of emotions. It was a monumental achievement, a testament to human resilience.

However, it was also a stark reminder of the moral compromises they had made in the shadow of a brutal regime.

With each layer of rock they removed, it was as if they were unearthing the secrets of the mountain, revealing the dark underbelly of Trujillo's dominion over the land.

Enrique's voice grew stronger as he addressed his team once more. "This tunnel may be a symbol of Trujillo's power, but it's also a testament to our strength and unity. We are survivors, and we will endure. Our families are counting on us."

His words resonated with those around him, forging a sense of camaraderie among the laborers. As they toiled in the depths of the earth, the monumental tunnel stood as a symbol of their defiance, a testament to their determination to endure the darkest of times for the promise of a brighter future.

Enrique often found himself thinking about the day when they would finally be free, and their families would be safe. The tunnel they had constructed was more than just a passage through rock and earth; it was a passage to a better future, a future they had fought for and one that they would soon claim as their own.

33

CHAPTER

The colossal tunnel had become a testament to the endurance and determination of Mario, Enrique, and their team. It stretched deep into the heart of the mountain, a monument to the oppressive regime of Trujillo. With each passing day, as they labored to extract the precious gold, they came closer to completing their end of the dark deal.

However, the impending completion of their monumental task carried a heavy price—a debt to the dictator that they could not escape. The agreement had always been clear: their freedom would come at the cost of eventual deportation to Italy.

Enrique had known that this moment would arrive, that their bargain with the devil would demand its due. As he watched the final layers of rock being removed from the tunnel, he couldn't help but feel a sense of trepidation.

The day of his departure came without warning as if summoned by the whims of the regime. He was called to an austere office, his heart heavy with the knowledge of what awaited him. It was a somber scene, bathed in the dull glow of a single, flickering lightbulb.

In the cold, sterile atmosphere of the office, an official with a stern countenance handed Enrique a passport and a one-way ticket to Italy. The exchange was brisk and business-like, devoid of any room for discussion or the luxury of goodbyes. The oppressive regime, known for its lack of sentiment, orchestrated departures with an ironclad efficiency that allowed no room for emotional farewells. In those fleeting moments, Enrique felt the weight of leaving Isabella and little Mario behind, a burden that settled heavily on his heart.

As he accepted the passport, his thoughts raced back to the life he was leaving behind—the small house on Avenida Villaespesa, the aroma of Isabella's cooking, and the laughter of little Mario echoing through the rooms. The prospect of being separated from his family gnawed at him, leaving an indelible ache.

The official's impassive expression remained unchanged, indifferent to the personal struggles Enrique was enduring. With the documents in hand, Enrique knew that the course had been set, and he had no choice but to follow it. The words of parting stuck in his throat, unspoken and suppressed by the authoritarian air that surrounded him.

As Enrique walked towards the departure gate, his steps felt heavier with each passing moment. The awareness that he might not witness the everyday joys and milestones of his family's life intensified the sense of loss. Yet, he clung to the hope that this sacrifice would be temporary, that one day, they would reunite and build a future together.

Boarding the plane, Enrique took a last, longing look at the Dominican landscape disappearing beneath the clouds. The lush greenery, the familiar cityscape, and the memories of his life in Santo Domingo blurred into a poignant farewell. Little did he know that this departure marked the beginning of a journey filled with uncertainty and challenges, a journey that would test the resilience of his spirit and the strength of his love for Isabella and Mario.

The promise of freedom was within his grasp, but it was bittersweet. The dictator's reach extended far beyond the island's shores, and Enrique knew that even in Italy, he would not be free from the specter of Trujillo.

The flight to Italy was a journey into the unknown, a stark contrast to the tunnels and mines of the Dominican Republic. It was a path that had been paved by sacrifice and compromise, a path that led him away from the land he had called home.

As the plane touched down on Italian soil, Enrique couldn't help but feel a sense of longing for his family and his homeland. The air smelled different here—crisp and foreign—and the bustling streets of Rome felt worlds away from the sun-drenched shores of Santo Domingo. He knew that his departure marked the end of one chapter and the beginning of another, but the specter of the colossal tunnel and the dictator's oppressive regime lingered in his thoughts, a shadow he couldn't shake.

The monumental tunnel and the work he had done in the depths of the earth would forever be a part of his history, a testament to the sacrifices made for the sake of family and freedom. In Italy, he would have to find a new path, a new way to support his loved ones, but the memories of the Dominican Republic and the monumental tunnel would always remain with him, a reminder of the resilience of the human spirit in the face of adversity.

34

CHAPTER

Enrique had barely touched down in Italy when a letter arrived, bearing the familiar seal of the Dominican Republic. He recognized the handwriting instantly—it was Isabella's. With trembling hands, he tore open the envelope, his heart pounding with dread.

As he read the words, a cold chill settled over him. The news was devastating—Mario's death in a helicopter crash during an exploration mission. The circumstances were shrouded in mystery, and the implications were ominous.

Tears welled up in Enrique's eyes as he read the letter, his emotions a tumultuous mix of grief and anger. It was a cruel twist of fate that had torn his beloved brother away from him, just as they were beginning to rebuild their lives.

"The crash... it wasn't an accident," Enrique whispered to himself, his voice choked with sorrow and disbelief. The more he read, the clearer it became that Mario's death was not a mere tragedy; it was a calculated act, designed to eliminate those who stood in the way of the regime's insatiable greed.

Enrique couldn't help but feel a seething anger building within him. The regime's reach extended even to Italy, and it seemed that no one was safe from its grasp. Mario's life had been taken, and it was clear that the oppressive regime would stop at nothing to secure its wealth and power.

As he put down the letter, Enrique's thoughts were consumed by a single determination: he would seek justice for his brother. Mario deserved more than to be a footnote in the dictator's dark history. He deserved to be remembered for the brave and dedicated soul he had been.

With a heavy heart, Enrique realized that he could not turn his back on his past. He had to confront the regime, uncover the truth behind Mario's death, and ensure that his brother's memory lived on.

The memory of his brother and the promise of justice fueled a new journey—one that would take him back to the Dominican Republic, back to the shadows of the colossal tunnel, to unravel the mysteries surrounding Mario's tragic end. It was a journey fraught with danger and uncertainty, but Enrique knew that he could not rest until he had unraveled the truth and sought retribution for his brother's untimely death.

"That's what my godfather was referring to," Tony whispered to himself, the words hanging in the air like a secret unveiled. His eyes were wide open, stunned and amazed at the profound truths he had just discovered within the pages of his grandfather's diary.

The rain outside seemed to echo the quiet intensity within Tony's mind. He traced the lines of the words on the aged pages, each revelation a drop in the vast sea of family history. The stories, once buried in the silence of the past, had found their voice, and Tony was the listener—a witness to the untold tales that had shaped his identity.

The rain tapped gently against the windowpanes of Tony's apartment in the Bronx, creating a soothing rhythm that enveloped the room. The soft glow of the lamp cast shadows on the walls, creating a cocoon of warmth and solitude. The air inside was filled with the earthy scent of rain, a comforting backdrop to the moment of revelation that had just unfolded.

Tony was alone in the dimly lit room, surrounded by the echoes of his grandfather's past. The pages of the diary lay open before him, filled with the handwritten accounts of a history that had been hidden, a story that had shaped the lives of those who came before him.

The room felt charged with the weight of the revelations. Tony's mind raced, connecting the dots between the whispers of the past and the present moment. The rain outside intensified as if nature itself were lending its voice to the unfolding narrative.

As Tony sat there, a myriad of emotions danced across his face—wonder, curiosity, and a deep sense of connection to the lineage that had paved the way for his existence. The raindrops on the window seemed to tap out a rhythm of continuity, a reminder that the stories within the diary were not isolated incidents but threads woven into the fabric of time.

The apartment, usually bustling with the sounds of the city, now held an almost sacred stillness. The revelations within the diary had cast a spell, transforming the mundane into the extraordinary. It was as if the room had become a sanctuary where the past and the present converged, where the legacy of his family unfolded like the petals of a long-forgotten flower.

In that quiet moment, Tony made a silent vow—to carry these stories forward, to be the bearer of the torch that illuminated the shadows of his family's history. The rain continued its

gentle symphony outside, providing a backdrop to Tony's introspection.

35

CHAPTER

Enrique had settled into his life in Italy, living with the ever-present memory of Mario and their shared dreams. The quest for justice for his brother had become the driving force in his life, guiding his every decision and keeping him focused on the path ahead.

One crisp morning, as the sun cast a warm glow over the Italian landscape in Florence, Enrique found himself at his small table, lost in thought. He had just finished his morning espresso when the familiar sound of a letter sliding through the mail slot broke the silence.

He reached for the envelope, and as he saw the familiar handwriting, his heart quickened. The sender was none other than Isabella. The very sight of her name filled him with both anticipation and longing.

With trembling hands, Enrique carefully opened the letter, his eyes scanning Isabella's words. It was a letter filled with news that would forever change their lives—a message of hope and promise.

"Enrique," the letter began, "I have the most incredible news to share with you. On Tuesday, the 30th of May 1961, a momentous event took place. Rafael Trujillo, the dictator who had cast a dark shadow over our lives, met his end in a violent ambush."

On that fateful night, the conspirators, armed with revolvers, pistols, a sawed-off shotgun, and rifles, positioned themselves strategically along the route that Trujillo was to take. The CIA, in their web of intrigue, had supplied some of these weapons. The meeting point was set near the Agua Luz Theater, on the highway leading to San Cristobal. By 8 pm, the assassins were in place, awaiting Trujillo's arrival.

At the stroke of 10 pm, Trujillo and his chauffeur embarked on their journey in the Chevrolet, heading towards the home of his girlfriend, Mona Sanchez. The conspirators chose a desolate stretch of road, where the shadows of palm trees concealed their presence. As Trujillo's car approached, Imbert, one of the conspirators, accelerated his vehicle in pursuit, the headlights cutting through the darkness like a predator stalking its prey.

The following minutes were a frenzy of bullets, with almost 30 piercing through Trujillo's car. In a desperate attempt to defend himself, Trujillo's chauffeur fired back with a machine gun.

Wounded and cornered, Trujillo exited the car, searching for his assailants. De la Maza and Imbert circled back, sealing Trujillo's fate. The ruthless act unfolded on that desolate road, and Trujillo fell, shot down by those who sought to free our land from his tyranny. His life ended on that very spot. In a macabre twist, the conspirators placed Trujillo's lifeless body in the trunk of a car, discreetly parking it two blocks away from the American consulate.

As Enrique read Isabella's words, he couldn't help but feel a wave of emotions welling up within him. Relief, mixed with disbelief, washed over him. The oppressive force that had torn their lives apart, the man who had haunted their dreams, was no more.

Isabella's letter continued, "The news of Trujillo's death has sent shockwaves through the Dominican Republic and beyond. The nation stands at a crossroads, teetering on the precipice of uncertainty, but also filled with hope for a brighter future."

With each word, Enrique's hope grew, and a newfound sense of purpose began to take root. Isabella went on to express her longing for their reunion. "I can hardly contain my excitement, Enrique. With Trujillo's reign of fear and oppression coming to an end, I dare to hope that we can be together again. The shadow that hung over us may finally be lifting."

Tears welled up in Enrique's eyes as he read those words. The prospect of seeing Isabella again, of being reunited after all they had endured, filled him with a profound sense of joy. The possibility of a future together, free from fear and oppression, was within their grasp.

As he read the final lines of the letter, Enrique's heart swelled with emotion. "I long to see you, to hold you in my arms once more," Isabella wrote. "Together, we can face the unknown with courage and determination. Our love has endured through the darkest of times, and now, there is hope on the horizon."

The world seemed to take on a new light as Enrique folded the letter, pressing it close to his heart. The fall of a tyrant had opened a door to a once-unimaginable future—a future where they could be together, where justice could be sought, and where the shadows of the past could finally begin to recede.

Enrique knew that the road ahead remained uncertain, but with Isabella's message of hope in his heart, he felt an unshakable determination. It was a promise that the past would no longer define their future, and that love and courage would guide their way.

With renewed purpose, Enrique looked out at the Italian landscape, a smile on his lips and a glint of hope in his eyes. The next chapter of their journey had just begun, and the possibilities were endless.

THE END or is it?